How many people could die suddenly and not leave even one embarrassing thing behind?

Had he swept it all away, knowing he was leaving, or had his life really been so bare?

Everything in his room was so neat and tidy. Was it all that simple for him—just get things in order and go? Had he ever hesitated, changed his mind, changed it back?

And now—what was he thinking, doing, feeling? Did he wonder about me, wonder what I was thinking, doing, feeling?

I turned slowly around, scowling at the neatness. All was in order. The only mess he'd left behind: my life.

ALSO AVAILABLE IN LAUREL-LEAF BOOKS:

WHIRLIGIG, *Paul Fleischman*
ANGELS ON THE ROOF, *Martha Moore*
UNDER THE MERMAID ANGEL, *Martha Moore*
RADIANCE DESCENDING, *Paula Fox*
THE SPIRIT WINDOW, *Joyce Sweeney*
KINSHIP, *Trudy Krisher*
SPITE FENCES, *Trudy Krisher*
THE WAR IN GEORGIA, *Jerrie Oughton*
LIFE IN THE FAT LANE, *Cherie Bennett*
A GIFT OF MAGIC, *Lois Duncan*

THIN ICE

MARSHA QUALEY

Published by
Bantam Doubleday Dell Books for Young Readers
a division of
Random House, Inc.
1540 Broadway
New York, New York 10036

ISBN: 0-440-22037-8

RL: 5.7

Reprinted by arrangement with Delacorte Press

Printed in the United States of America

December 1999

10 9 8 7 6 5 4 3 2

OPM

THIN
ICE

PART 1

Three hours into my birthday party, people were jumping off the roof. This was not dangerous, just dumb. It wasn't dangerous because we'd had three blizzards in ten days and the snow had drifted high against the house, almost to the eaves.

But it was dumb because by three hours into the party the temperature had dropped to ten above. Though their necks were probably safe from being broken, people risked frostbite. Come to think of it, that's dangerous, too.

I don't know who had the idea to rev up my party with roof jumping. Probably the idea came from no one in particular, just got born out of the atmosphere—one of those inspirations brewed out of the combination of music, dancing, and chip dip. Before anyone had gathered her wits to say "That's stupid," about twenty people—old and young, my friends and my brother's—had filed outside.

The jumpers left doors open, and the exchange of cold air for hot was welcome. So was the extra room. Our house isn't that big, and at one point I had counted fifty people. That was early on, and guests kept coming.

The roof jumping didn't last long. No one could find a ladder, so the only way to get on the roof was to climb up the drift. It was packed down quickly, what with twenty people jumping up and mostly falling short. But a few lucky fools made it, and I guess they must have thought the jumping was fun because someone got the bright idea to throw the birthday girl off the roof. I was in the kitchen hiding from my best friends, the twins, who wanted to make me a middleman in their newest juggling trick, which involved knives. Keeping one eye out for the twins, I was watching all the outside activity through the window when the jumpers came for me. I should have read minds, should have seen it coming. I *did* see all this huddling and laughing and everyone suddenly turning to look at me. Then five or six of them rushed inside.

"No, no!" I shrieked as I was picked up, arms and legs.

"Help, help!" I called as I was hauled out of the house, my butt swinging and bumping against every possible thing.

My brother just grinned and watched, no help at all. But then, I'm sure there have been plenty of times in our life together when he's wanted to do something just like that to me—no doubt without the landing cushion of snow.

All the Einsteins present, no one could figure out how to get me up on the roof. It was just as well, because by then the drift was really packed down and the dumb idea had turned dangerous. They dropped me. The legs around me shifted, left, right. I rolled, picked up snow, and fast as I could, started stuffing it up the pants of my tormentors. No Einstein myself, I was on my knees when I began my attack and so unable to flee. Retribution was certain. I prepared to take it, maybe in the face. Or down the neck. But right then the loud siren and flashing lights of a cop car did what the January night hadn't: froze us.

The cruiser turned a corner a block away and headed toward my house.

"Who called the cops?" people asked each other.

I frowned. A complaint didn't make sense. The music wasn't that loud, it wasn't even midnight, and there were only three houses on the street. Besides, all the neighbors were at the party.

"Must be the light," someone said, and we all looked toward the driveway. My brother was a mechanic at a car dealership and he had borrowed the owner's spotlight, one of those monster beamers that twirl around and light up the sky. It was parked in the driveway, a zillion watts aimed heaven-high. It wasn't rotating, though. Scott had fixed the beam so it shone on a huge bunch of helium-filled balloons.

The jumpers and I went inside and waited. Everyone quieted, listening for the bell.

Two rings. Scott opened the door and motioned the officer inside. It was Al Walker, an old friend of my brother's. A good guy, and I'd always liked him. Amazing, though, how a uniform and gun can alter someone's appearance.

Al walked in, nodded to my brother. "Town ordinance, Scott. That spotlight should have gone off at eleven."

"Sorry. I'll do it now."

Al the Cop smiled at everyone and walked into the living room. His head ratcheted around on his neck. Checking for beer, I guessed. He came over to me.

"Seventeen, Arden?"

"That's right."

"Well, I'm glad I got off duty in time to extend my good wishes." And like an old car getting a jump start, the crowd roared back to life as his six feet four inches kind of curled around my five feet two and he laid one on me. Lips.

Kissed by a cop.

Happy birthday, Arden. Happy birthday to me.

I know more about my family than I remember. I know I was six and at home with a baby-sitter when my parents were killed in a plane crash in Central America. They were doctors, volunteering for a few weeks at a rural clinic. I know that Scott, my only sibling, was away at college. I know he rushed home to be with me.

I know we had no relatives and that one or two old friends of my parents' emerged from somewhere far away and offered to take me so Scott could return to school. I know he refused the offers and instead moved back to Penokee and enrolled at the technical college in Superior. I know there was plenty of money left for us both, enough to pay for the house and for someone to watch me while he was at school. I know we went through a lot of baby-sitters. I know that Scott, after finishing school, got a job fixing cars. I know he dated, but I don't know names. I know I got older and he did too. I know it couldn't have been fun, being mother and father to a younger sister.

I *remember* bits. My mother's unruly hair slipping out of a scarf. My father's hairy hands curled over mine as we'd swing a baseball bat. Singing in the car. A tent and a campfire. Smoky smell of a scratchy sweater. Bits.

I remember story times. If I want to conjure up my parents, to remember a touch, a voice, a smell, it helps to think about *The Sailor Dog*, or *Betsy-Tacy*, or *Frog and Toad*.

I know I had nightmares. I remember waking up shivering and screaming, wet with tears and sweat. I remember once Scott burst into my room. He held me and whispered, "It's okay, it's okay."

I remember him saying, "I have dreams too."

That helped. Comforted me most of all, maybe, to know that those pictures in my head of flames and ripped metal also haunted my brother.

I know we were watched by people who cared about us and by people with power to split us apart. I remember talks with school counselors, who always liked to take my hand and ask questions: How are you? What did you eat for breakfast? Do you need help shopping for *personal* things?

They never asked what they really wanted to know:

Does your brother bring home girlfriends? Does he drink and do drugs? Does he ever touch you?

No, no, and no.

With time my nightmares went away. And so did people's questions. I guess everyone got used to us. And now, most of the time, it feels like we've always lived this way: Scott and Arden. Brother and sister. The Munros. Family of two.

There's a limited view from my bedroom window. I see the front yard and the end of the driveway. I see the twins' house, and the windows of their separate bedrooms. Blue-striped curtains for Kady, tie-dyed sheet for Jean. Beyond their house, rising above everything, there's the omnipresent plume of polluted industrial exhaust from the paper mill downriver.

This is northern Wisconsin, so of course I see plenty of trees—pine, oak, poplar, and birch. A lilac bush.

The morning after the party, aroused by an unidentifiable noise from a deep slumber, I saw two guys hopping out of a pickup. One spotted me and waved. I didn't want to seem churlish and waved back.

They'd come for the spotlight. Scott went out and shook hands, even slapped one of them on the shoulders. Weird how I've never seen a girl do that: shake, shake, how ya doing, whack.

Scott was dressed for playing outside: snowmobile suit and huge boots. He stood around until the spotlight guys were gone; then he disappeared. I heard the rumble of a snowmobile, his new toy. The sled's engine roared; then the sound faded as he drove into the woods behind our house. We live at the edge of town, just a quarter mile from a state forest and its miles of trails. He'd be gone all day.

A horrible thought invaded my sleepy brain: Was I left with the party mess?

When I need to, I can move. I jumped out of bed and hustled to the kitchen.

Spotless.

Living room?

Immaculate.

While I slept, he had cleaned. What a guy, my brother.

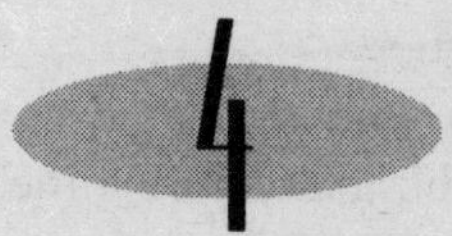

I spent the morning in my workshop in the basement. Ten years ago, when Scott and I became the sole occupants of this house, we pretty much left things as they had been: Our parents' stuff stayed in their room; their paintings and photographs stayed on the living room walls; their CDs remained stacked by the stereo. The basement too had been their domain. There was a small medical library, a huge desk, and several file cabinets. More pictures, tools, and a few pieces of beat-up furniture.

Like a creeping weed, Scott and I took over the house. The life my parents had planted became overgrown with our stuff. First, Scott moved into the big bedroom, claiming the private bathroom with its whirlpool tub. Then our posters and music started to fill the living room. We stashed their pictures and knickknacks and sold the furniture the year I was in fifth grade, and for months the living room was empty except for some metal shelving, the TV and stereo system, and a futon, the first in Penokee. Then Scott hired a cabinetmaker, and now we have all this custom-made oak stuff. There's a new futon.

I took over the basement. I figured it was fair because he got the great bathtub. The biggest room has been pretty much a clubhouse for me and the twins and any current friends. There's even a black curtain strung across one end, a backdrop for juggling shows.

The back room is mine, all mine. Knock before entering. My workshop.

I make picture frames. This is more than a hobby, it's art. And it's business. During the last few years I'd made a nice chunk of change from selling my frames through gift shops in the area. No lie. My stuff is good—northwoods folk art with an edge. And I'd recently branched out, added on mirrors and earring stands. I'm legit: The first summer my stuff was selling in shops, Scott hauled me off to a lawyer and I registered as a bona fide business. ArdenArt.

I made my first frame at camp the summer after fifth grade—cardboard, painted macaroni, a whole bottle of glue. Pretty lame.

But it must have been fun, because when I got home I started gluing painted Popsicle sticks together into rectangles and decorating them. Most of my creations fell apart, but one, decorated with acorns and seed pods, caught the eye of the cabinetmaker who was measuring the living room for bookshelves. He showed me how to use a saw and a miter box, where to glue, when to nail or screw. I took some classes on using power tools, and the rest—glass cutting, matting, staining—I learned from books.

Lately I'd been working with costume jewelry. Last summer I foraged all the garage sales and flea markets and came away with boxes of cheap, flashy baubles to mount on birch and cherry frames. Rhinestones on dark cherry sell the best.

It's tricky, though. Not just a matter of glue. You have to carefully rout a hole in the molding that approximates the shape of the stone. I don't just glue the stones onto the surface, I inlay. Careful touch required. My parents were both surgeons. I have their hands.

It's easy to get lost in work you love. Oblivious. I was setting a bar of fake rubies when a shadow fell over the table. Instead of plucking the stone, the tweezers I was using jabbed into my palm.

Watch your mouth, Arden.

"Did I disturb you?" Jean asked.

I held up my hand to show her the tiny bubble of blood.

"Sorry. Have you had a tetanus shot? Those tweezers look rusty."

"Lucky for you, yes. Don't sneak up on me like that."

"I knocked. You didn't hear?"

"Obviously not."

"Want lunch? Kady's fixing something."

I looked out the small window. Nothing to see but snow. "I'm hungry, but not enough to put on boots and a coat. I'll make a sandwich."

"She's *here*. We thought there might be leftovers from the party."

My stomach rumbled. It's a hard noise to ignore, and I seldom do, which is maybe one reason I'm a size eleven.

At least sixty people had been eating nonstop for four hours last night; even so, there were leftovers. Kady had the kitchen table covered with food—salads, cake, bread, cheeses, spreads, and soda. We denied ourselves nothing.

"Great party last night," said Kady, just before biting into a sandwich. Mayo and mustard oozed out, coating the corner of her mouth.

"The best ever," said Jean, and she blew across the long neck of a root-beer bottle. "We've got four older brothers and not one of them even gives a birthday present, much less a party."

With my little finger, I scraped and lifted a red rose off the cake. Licked it with my tongue. "If you have to be orphaned and raised by a brother," I said, "be sure it's one who can throw a blowout."

"Where is he?" Jean asked.

"Snowmobiling." They both made a face, and I laughed. Then they both made another face, and I laughed again. "You should see yourselves," I said.

Fraternal twins, they didn't look a bit alike. Some people have even said Jean and I, with our auburn hair and fair skin, look more like sisters. Jean and Kady act like twins, though. Facial expressions, mannerisms, utterances—identical. They move, speak, and breathe just alike. Maybe that's the result of five years of juggling, of all those hours spent practicing the precise motions needed to toss and catch the pins, dolls, balls, and other odd stuff they use in their act. Or maybe it's the other way: maybe they're so good at juggling because they have this innate togetherness. Synchronicity.

I move alone. Artists do, right?

"I've only been on a snowmobile once," Jean said.

Kady shook her head. "Too loud."

"I think it looks kind of fun," I said. "All that speed."

"What would be fun," said Jean, "is this." She pulled a folded newspaper page from her hip pocket and laid it on the table within my reach. She and her sister exchanged identical looks—two brows furrowed, two mouths set.

NORTHLAND WINTER FESTIVALS. Penokee's annual winter carnival was highlighted, with a photo of last year's award-winning snow sculpture.

I shrugged. "Same old stuff. The usual crowds, ski races, and traffic. What's fun?"

"It gave us this idea," said Kady. "We want you in on it."

"Not that we like you," Jean added, "but because you have a car."

I tossed a slimy pasta shell at her. "Go eat at home."

Kady leaned forward. Her elbow pressed into a half-eaten whole wheat bun. "When summer comes, let's go on the road. We'll hit all the festivals and craft fairs. We'll do our show and you can set up a kiosk with your stuff. Think of the money you can make if you don't have to give a percentage to store owners."

I frowned. "I make plenty now. Besides, I bet it takes a vendor's permit or something."

"That's why we start now," Kady said. "We do it right: We get in touch with the organizers in each town and apply. You send your portfolio and we send our audition tape. Give them references, pay a vendor's fee, whatever it takes."

"Traveling from town to town," Jean said. "We'll be gypsies."

I squinted. "You mean geep-seez."

"Yahs, geep-seez," she answered.

Kady snorted. "What sort of accent is that supposed to be?"

"Geep-see," I said.

"Well, cut it out," she answered. "Aside from being annoying, I suspect it demeans someone."

I turned and looked at Jean, my eyes wide. "And who says I don't have a mother?"

She nodded. "Lucky me. I have two."

"So what do you say?" Kady asked me.

I scooped another rose and sucked it off my finger. "I think—"

"Yahs," said Jean, "she teenks—"

Kady flicked an olive pit at her twin.

"I think it's the best idea ever."

After eating, we talked and outlined details. The economy of this part of Wisconsin depends on tourists, and every little burg fabricates some reason to throw a town party in the summer, sometimes another one in winter. Lumberjack Days, Miner Days, Muskie Mania, Voyageur Fest. My favorite—Blueberry Bonanza, a three-day celebration right here in Penokee in July.

"The only question," said Kady, "is whether we should try to market the hourlong show or the half-hour."

"Kids can't sit for long," Jean argued. "Especially if it's hot."

"They'll sit for us," said Kady. "We're good. And the longer the show, the bigger our fee."

"Who books the acts and pays, do you think?" I asked. "Chamber of Commerce? I bet some of those towns are too small to have one."

Jean shook her head. "I'm discouraged already. Too many details. We'll never get it together. Even if we do, they'll never hire kids."

"You're always so pessimistic," Kady said.

"Am not."

"Isn't she?" I was asked.

I haven't stayed friends with the two of them by taking sides. I just smiled.

"Well?" Kady persisted. "Isn't she?"

The phone rang and it was a welcome sound. "Whatever she is," I replied, rising, "she's your twin."

"Geep-see house," I hissed into the phone. Jean laughed; Kady rolled her eyes.

A pause on the line, breathing. Then: "Arden?" Male, older, befuddled.

"Sorry. Yes, this is Arden."

"Al Walker." Al the Cop. Did he want to kiss me again?

"Arden, are you alone? Do you drive? Never mind, I'll get you."

"Why? What's up?"

"Arden . . . bad news. Scott . . . the river . . . his sled . . . there's been an accident."

6

Scott wasn't dead, but it took Al a long time to spit that out. Babbling, sputtering, incoherent, the competent cop was hysterical about his friend's accident. I hung up and turned to Kady and Jean. "My brother's been hurt. He's in the hospital in Ashland. It sounds bad." I turned this way and that, trying to find keys, hat, boots. I managed to bump into Jean, who had started clearing the table. Carrot sticks torpedoed across the kitchen.

Kady lifted my key chain off its hook by the telephone. "I'll drive, you worry."

Scott was in an ER cubicle. I burst through an opening in the starched curtains, expecting bandages, tubes, blood, doctors.

My brother was alone, lying under a pile of blankets. His hands were thrust into the air, holding a worn magazine. *Sports Illustrated,* an old swimsuit issue.

I sat on the bed, bouncing it. He took a last look at the magazine, then let it drop on his stomach. There was a small solitary bandage just above his eyebrow.

"How are you? What happened?"

"Did you bring my clothes?"

"No. Was I supposed to?"

A snarly noise climbed out of his throat. "Didn't Al tell you?"

"He could barely get his name out."

Scott nodded. "I guess he was still scared."

"He scared me. He was hysterical. Listening to him, I thought you'd bought it."

"Almost did."

I picked up the magazine and riffled the pages, animating the models. Not a single size eleven. "Almost dead, but you still have the strength to ogle babes." I dropped the magazine and it slid off the bed onto the floor. "What happened, Scott?"

A nurse entered the cubicle. I stepped aside as she performed nurse work. "Lookin' good!" she said finally. "Body temp is up. Other vitals are normal. Another hour or two and I bet we let you out of here." She turned to me. "Are you the sister?"

The sister. I nodded.

"You have a lucky brother."

The snarly noise again, then: "She has a stupid brother."

The nurse patted Scott's shoulder and left. Neither of us spoke. Voices from the waiting area filtered in.

Scott was twenty-nine and balding. A hand-sized patch of pink scalp had extended his forehead. He's only a few inches taller than me, with the same tree-trunk solidity, and the same incongruously long, sinewy fingers. Perfect for an artist. Perfect for a mechanic. Perfect for a surgeon, which was the goal he had been pursuing when he changed his life to take care of me.

His hand raked the hair surrounding the pink patch, then dropped to the bed. I picked it up and squeezed. "I'll cook tonight."

He was skeptical. "Leftovers?"

"Anything. What do you want?"

He nestled down, pulling blankets up to his chin. Ruddy face, tufts of dark hair amid the hospital white. "I want my snowmobile back."

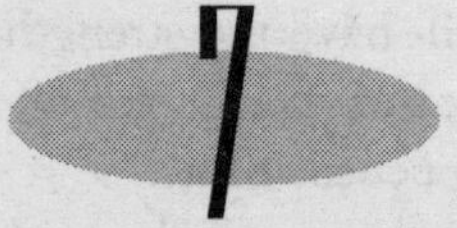

His sled was at the bottom of the Gogebic River, he said, about five miles north of the dam. The Gogebic's a deep, fast-moving river that flows through Penokee on its way to Lake Superior, forty miles north.

"I met the guys at Winker's Tavern. We had a few beers, then decided to head back to town."

"Were you drunk? You don't drink."

"Don't I?" he snapped.

I stood and crossed my arms. "Then what happened?"

"One of the guys wanted to follow the river back to town. It's a lot shorter than the forest trail."

"But not as safe," I said.

"Obviously not." He closed his eyes. "We went single file. Al was last, I was right ahead of him. The ice is pretty thick, but the current is strong underneath. I was watching the guys ahead, they were really gunning it. I wanted to, but, geez, I've only had the sled two weeks, I wasn't that sure of what I was doing. And I was feeling the beers, so I thought I'd better take it easy. They were just flying." He drew up his knees, making a hummock of white flannel. "All of a sudden there was this gap in the ice. Stupid, cautious me—I wasn't carrying enough speed to get over it. Al passed me then. He just blew over it. I looked at him, looked at the hole, next thing I knew, I was sliding into water."

I sat and took his hand.

The story continued. He caught the edge of the ice—the collision knocking out his breath but tearing him off the machine, which bobbed for a moment before sliding down through the water. He hung on to the edge of the ice, watching it crack further while he felt his bulky suit bubble up, buoying him. "The ice cracked and loosened every time I moved," Scott said. "I couldn't haul myself out." His hands tightened and curled, eyes squeezed closed as he replayed the struggle. "Al looked back and saw it happen. He circled around, got a rope out of his crash kit and pulled me onto the ice. Then he got me out of the wet suit, threw me on the back of his sled, and hauled me to the highway. Flagged down a car, and here I am."

Scott opened his eyes and smiled. "Al was manic—jumping up and down on the highway, screaming, flashing his badge to stop the car . . ."

"So you weren't hurt? Hypothermia, is that why you're here?"

"I'm okay. Brush with death, but nothing a few heated blankets didn't fix."

He was the one who nearly froze, but *I* was numb. Winter water kills. If he'd hit his head or not jumped in time or had been dragged under by the sled or if Al hadn't thought to look . . .

The *what ifs?* were a terror.

"Like you said, I nearly bought it." My brother shook his head, disgusted. "Next time out," he said, "I pump some speed."

Next time?

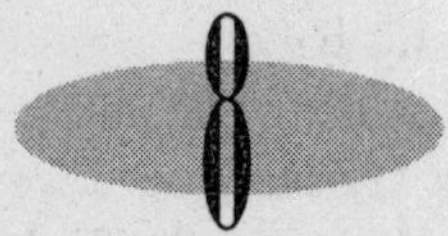

"No calls. I don't want to talk to anyone."

Made sense to me. Come that close to dying, a person probably wanted a little time to let his thoughts jell.

The phone had been ringing off the hook since we got home from the hospital and I was tired of answering and explaining, so I taped a new message:

Thanks for calling, Scott is fine. Leave a message, and we'll get back to you when we have thawed.

"Or do you think I should I have said *defrosted?*"

Scott didn't find that funny. Just looked at me and made a face. Just lifted his hand in a little blow-off wave. *Shut up, Arden.*

All evening we screened the messages. His friends called with advice about getting the sled towed out, my friends called with pleas to know more, Scott's boss called and told him to take a few days off. The twins' mom, Mrs. Drummond, called with an offer of food. "I made too much lasagna. I don't want to bother you, so Jean will just run across and leave it in the breezeway."

By ten the messages had dwindled. I was in the kitchen cleaning up when I heard my brother talking on the phone. I automatically tuned out. Over the years we've learned to give each other space. In some ways, two people living together have a lot less privacy than a large family like the Drummonds, where so much is going on that a lot goes unnoticed.

I was feeding potato salad to the disposal when Scott appeared. "I'm going out," he said.

"This late?"

"Yeah, this late."

"Where?"

He made another face, gave another little dismissal with his hand. "Just for an hour. Go to bed, okay? Or study. Don't you always have a bio test on Mondays?"

This was true, and how like him to remember. Only hours after nearly dying in icy water, my brother was checking on my schoolwork.

"I'm in good shape. Protein synthesis. Easy. Where are you going?"

He looked at me hard. We rarely asked that of each

other. Usually the information was offered, but seldom requested. I rephrased the question. "Why are you going out, Scott? You should go to bed. Stay inside and stay warm, that's what the nurse said."

His face softened and relaxed. He chewed on his lip. I could see some sort of struggle going on. "I'm going to see my girlfriend."

A girlfriend? Well, blow me over. "Huh? Since when?"

He grinned, pleased with himself, enjoying my surprise. "She was at the party, Arden. I introduced you."

Eyes closed, I scanned the party picture. Then I knew. "The tall blonde in the navy sweater. Has to be her because she laughed at your mechanic jokes."

He nodded.

"Name?"

"Claire Poole."

"How old is she? What does she do?"

"You should have paid attention when you had the chance. I'll be home by midnight."

He slipped into a jacket and left it unzipped. No gloves, no hat.

"Won't you get cold?" I asked.

He twirled his key ring on his finger and opened the door. "Midnight," he repeated. Before the door had even closed, I heard him swear, heard something hit the door, heard metal and body crash on the concrete steps. I got there just as he was lifting a covered cake pan out of the snow by the stoop. Lasagna.

I don't know if Scott got home by midnight, but he was there when I left for school the next day. He hadn't changed, and if I hadn't seen him go out I would have thought he had never budged from the chair in the living room. Brooding look, tousled hair, rumpled clothing. Must be love.

"Nice date with the girlfriend?" I asked.

"Fine," he whispered.

"Going to work?"

He shook his head.

"Need a blanket? Should I turn up the heat?"

Shook his head again.

"I'll be home right away today."

He managed a smile. "Whatever. See you at supper."

At school, I expected to be swamped by everyone's curiosity about my brother's accident. After all, it was just the sort of news people in this town love: a near-death experience involving a snowmobile.

Old news already, I guess. During the short walk across the parking lot and through the halls to my locker, all I got was:

"Arden, did you study for bio?"

"See my new shoes?"

"Gawd, I slept late. Talk later."

"Give this note to Ryan, okay?"

"Is that a new shirt?"

No, it wasn't a new shirt. Bought it old, in fact. Three-fifty at Ragstock over in Duluth. Pearl snaps and black piping to contrast with the red gingham. And of course, the five-inch "Morrie" embroidered in cursive above the breast pocket.

The bio test, fourth hour, was a breeze, but I could tell others were sweating. I finished early and used the extra time to sketch frame designs. My notebooks are filled with them. Some of my best frames have been inspired by the dullness of school.

Just before lunch, Mrs. Richter handed out last week's test. Bio was my best class, and I wasn't too worried. There it was—big blue A.

"Nice work, Arden," she said.

"Yes," I answered. "My parents will be so pleased."

The teacher paused, then shrugged, letting it pass.

No big blue A the rest of the day, anywhere. Just an overload of mind-numbing information. The real crippler came at the end of the day during world history when Ms. Penny returned a test. D plus. I moaned, and the teacher paused in her determined stroll down the aisle where she was dusting us with test papers.

"Yes, Arden?"

"D plus," I said. "My parents will kill me."

She stared evenly. "Old joke, Arden. But you're right, they would, *if* they were alive."

Ow, she's a tough one, that Ms. Penny. The instant the bell rang, I was gone, D plus stuffed into my book bag.

Scott seldom hassled me about grades. He praised the good ones, shrugged over the bad ones. "She knows what's going on," he once said to a teacher at conference. "She'll straighten up when she's ready."

Ready or not, that history grade was lower than I wanted. I didn't intend to go to the nearby community college. I was meant for the art school down in Minneapolis, or one out East. The old GPA was important. My ticket out of town.

"Extra credit, Arden," I ordered myself. "And no workshop tonight until you study."

Scott was still in the chair. Darkness comes early in winter, and I didn't see him until I switched on the light.

"Whoa—hello!" I said.

Dead or alive? His eyes were closed. For a moment I was heated with thoughts about delayed shock, maybe cardiac arrest.

His eyes rolled open, which was almost as startling as finding his still body in the dark.

"You scared me!"

"By sitting here?"

"Yes, by sitting there. Haven't you moved all day?"

"To the bathroom. Kitchen. I had a sandwich." His eyes closed. "Arden," he whispered, "if I had died, you'd be okay, wouldn't you?"

"No, I wouldn't. I'd be . . . it would be awful, Scott. What a crazy thing to say."

His thumbs tapped on the chair arm and he looked

around. "What I mean is, you don't really need me. Things are in order. They have been for years. Christ, I was probably the only twenty-year-old in the history of the world who made out a will. Mom and Dad left plenty of money, the Drummonds are there for you, you're almost done with school."

"Don't even talk about it, Scott."

"If Al hadn't pulled me out—"

"He did pull you out. You're okay, Scott. It was a close one, but nothing really happened. Don't worry. Everything's okay."

He massaged his forehead. His lips moved.

"What?" I asked.

He waved me away. I went to the kitchen to fix a snack. Later, when I thought about it all, I realized he *had* spoken.

Barely a whisper, but he'd said, "Everything's changed."

When it's only two people living together, things can get pretty intense, so you figure out how to keep some distance. Closing the bedroom door works. I closed mine and attacked my homework. When the powerful growls of my stomach drove me out of the room an hour later, the first thing I saw was Scott, still slumped in his chair and brooding in the dark room. He barely lifted his hand in greeting when I walked in.

Cheer up already, I thought. I said, "Should we order pizza?"

He did that little hand flip again, and I must have leaked a snort or a tsk or something because he looked up at me and said, "Back off."

Breathing room. After devouring more of the party leftovers, I went down to the basement. A gift shop in Duluth wanted a batch of mirrors and earring stands and I was behind on the order. I cut molding and glued wood until the dust and fumes threatened to make me loopy. At ten-thirty, when I finally started cleaning up, I heard banging and thumping and voices from the garage. I hoped it wasn't the girlfriend he was entertaining up there. We both had better manners than that.

Scott and one of his work buddies were in the garage. Reuben greeted me. "Hey, Arden, you're an artist, right? Doesn't this look like a fancy modern art sculpture?"

A battered pile of metal and plastic was heaped on the ground where it had slid off the tilted bed of a tow truck. My brother's snowmobile, salvaged from the river.

"Sure does, Reuben. You could probably get a few thousand for it down in Minneapolis, especially with the right title." We joked around with titles for a bit while Scott poked and pulled at the machine. Then he gave it a final kick and swore. "Come in for cocoa?" I asked Reuben. Someone had to be pleasant.

"Nope. It's late. Time to head home." He pulled gloves out of a jacket pocket and whacked them on Scott's shoulder. "Must make you feel lucky to look at that heap, Scotty. After a day of rocking around in the river, think how banged up you'd've been."

Scott smiled. "It's crossed my mind." He reached into his hip pocket and pulled out a wallet, slid some bills out. "They can't possibly pay you enough for the after-hours work, Reuben. Here's something you don't need to tell the taxman about."

"Wait till you see your copy of the insurance claim. The diver's bill alone goes over a thousand."

Scott nodded, but my jaw dropped. "What?" I said.

Reuben smiled at my surprise. "Gosh, yeah. The recovery part of the claim will be over fifteen hundred, easy." He pushed the bills back at Scott. "I'll get my share, Scotty. No tip necessary. But you can do one thing for me—I'd love to take a look at the 'Cuda. Didn't you put in new front seats last fall?"

Scott grinned, bad mood immediately erased, and he nodded and led Reuben to the back of the garage, to a sky-blue mound. Scott grabbed hold of the blue cotton and whipped it off in a single, masterful sweep, revealing his pride and joy, his treasure, his mistress, and the reason this two-person household has a four-car garage: a carefully restored 1970 Plymouth Barracuda.

My brother's passion was not mine. He saw automotive perfection. I saw a squat old green car. He started his spiel: 383 Magnum . . . pistol grip . . . Weld-wheels . . .

I'd heard it before and my feet were cold. Time to take sanctuary in the kitchen.

"Does insurance really cover your accident?" I asked him later, when Reuben had gone and we were both in the kitchen warming up with cocoa. Immediately I wished I hadn't asked. The good mood he'd developed from showing off the car vanished as he thought about the snowmobile.

"Yes, really. The policy has coverage for stupidity."

This self-flagellation was tiresome, and I must have made a noise. He looked at me sharply. "I'm not proud of what I did, Arden. It was an expensive, stupid, scary mistake." He dropped within himself again, his favorite place lately. "A big fat mistake," he whispered. "Allow me to be mad at myself."

I had nothing to say, he didn't want to talk to me, but neither of us wanted to back off first, so thank gawd for the phone. It rang, I answered, she said hello. I debated taking advantage of his torpor and talking to her myself. I was dying to ask a few questions—age, occupation, intentions—but, bright girl that I am, I figured doing that would only steam him further.

"Of course it's not too late," I said sweetly. "One moment, please."

12

Over the next few days I cannibalized the snowmobile wreck. Scott and the insurance company saw a total loss, Reuben saw a goofy sculpture, but I saw raw material for ArdenArt. I was inspired: I'd broaden my markets and reach out to the northwoods male with a line of crushed-metal frames and mirrors.

While I ripped apart the old toy, Scott began work on the hard job of buying a new one. Evidently this takes planning and research. Four days had passed since his dunk in the Gogebic and he still hadn't gone back to work. He had, however, managed to get to Ed's Stop and Shop, the nearest c-store, to pick up a stack of snowmobiling magazines.

"I want the right one this time," he said when we met in the kitchen Thursday evening. I opened the refrigerator and grabbed a container of party leftovers. One more meal? I opened and sniffed. Yes, maybe so.

"With this machine I want power. I want speed. I want—"

I sniffed the air. "Gosh, what's the funny smell? Why, it's . . . it's . . . testosterone!"

He made a face, then yanked the refrigerator open and pulled out his own container of leftovers. We sat at the table with spoons and plastic tubs and had supper.

"If you don't go back to work, Scott, you won't be able to afford any new toys."

"I've got plenty of vacation time logged. But you'll be pleased to know that I'm going in for the day tomorrow."

"Only one day?"

"Wyatt Pierce is bringing in his car and he won't let anyone else touch it."

"The bedeviled Mercedes? Well, you are the vintage-car specialist. Do you get paid extra when someone asks for you especially?"

"Nothing extra and I'm getting tired of it. I should open my own shop. Lorenzo Motors would realize pretty quickly what I was worth."

"Why don't you? Do it right here in town, then you wouldn't have to commute sixty miles every day."

"Scott's Auto Repair in Penokee, Wisconsin—now there's a dream come true."

Phone. Figuring it would be one of my many admirers, I moved to answer, but he held me back. "We're not home?" I asked.

He shook his head, let the phone ring three more times, then relented and answered himself. "Yeah? Oh, hi."

Even with his cryptic responses, I could tell soon enough that it was Claire. I should have done the courteous thing and gone to another room, but watching and listening to him was too interesting. Besides, if he had wanted privacy he could have moved to another phone. I decided that maybe he wanted me to pay attention—perhaps he was offering a lesson in relationships.

I kept one eye on him as I thumbed through his magazines. The ads were full of happy people dressed in bulky clothing. My brother didn't look too happy. His face was a study. I saw distress, and maybe some other emotion. Love?

After he hung up he stood mannequin-still. Then his fingers started a rhythmic tapping on the counter. I tapped along on the table, but either he didn't notice or he didn't care. "Ahem," I said. "Should I assume you're going out tonight?"

He walked away without bothering to answer.

13

He didn't go out, but spent the night in his room. And the next morning, for the first time since he'd slid into the icy Gogebic River, he went to work.

By afternoon I felt like I'd had my own slide into cold water. At school, Jean told me our movie plans were off because her whole family was going down to Eau Claire. Something to do with a college friend of her mother's and a crisis. "Why the whole family?" I asked.

"Mom will hold hands and we'll go shopping. Dad's picking us up right after school, so we don't need a ride." Mr. Drummond was the principal at the elementary school across the street from the high school. The twins usually rode with him in the morning and went home with me. Jean dumped her lunch bag on my tray and left. Seniors had early lunch, and she'd only hung around to dump the news.

After she left, I looked around the cafeteria, wondering who in that huge assembly of six hundred students might offer the key to a good time. I passed over the freshmen and sophomores (I wasn't that desperate), looked at the backs of the departing seniors, then picked up my tray and moved over to a table of classmates. Leesa Coltrane was holding court. Unless you liked endless conversations about clothing, Leesa was not the world's most interesting person, but she did throw parties. The conversation—shoes, the latest Delia's catalog, Ms. Penny's wicked grading system—didn't even slow down when I arrived, though Cody Rock managed to stop stroking some sophomore girl's hair long enough to give a little wave.

I can't say I'm real close to many of the kids in school. They're all mostly party friends, I guess. One hundred sixty-seven classmates and I've known many of them most of my life; except for Jean and Kady, there's no one I automatically think of as a good friend. How did this happen? How does a person get to be seventeen and have so few friends? In a crisis, who would come hold my hand?

"Gawd, Arden, you wear the weirdest clothes." Leesa smiled and bit down on a baby carrot. "Where did you get that shirt?"

I was wearing my second-best, a kiwi-colored bowling shirt formerly owned by "Franz." "Duluth."

"The *mall*?"

"Ragstock."

She made a face and a tiny orange sliver popped out of her mouth and stuck to her lip.

"Ragstock?" said Tiffanee. "That's where I went for a Halloween costume. There was such a weird clerk there. He had hair that hadn't been combed for like a year and he smelled."

Everyone looked at me and my shirt as if we gave off a bad scent. It didn't, nor did I. I'm clean and I use color-safe bleach in the laundry.

"I like it," said Cody. "But maybe you should leave a few more buttons undone."

What a wit! As the others laughed, Cody turned to his girl and they smacked a quick kiss, a young lovers' high five.

The conversation got off me and back on track and I gleaned that everyone's life this weekend was centering around either work or a hockey game in Superior. No party.

Friday night alone. Well, I could work or study, right?

The house was dark and cold when I got home. My mood exactly.

The first order of business was food. As I opened the fridge the phone rang, and my spirits soared. Had I won something? Was there a party? Had the Drummonds changed plans and stayed home?

It was my brother. "Hey, sis, I need a favor."

"I just got home. Can I eat first?"

"Quit whining, this will only take a minute. I'm having a hell of a time with the valves on this Mercedes. I came home at lunch and shot off a question to one of the guys on the mech list. Check and see if there's a reply."

The mech list was an Internet group of car mechanics who used the list to share information. I'm no Luddite, but I'm not exactly in love with the computer. I mess around with it some, though not as much as my brother. For a while I used it to network with other crafters, but I got fed up with the way newsgroup and bulletin board discussions digressed—there were too many middle-aged women obsessing over muffins or their gardens. Scott, however, loved what he found through the Internet and he especially loved the hardware. Every year he'd power up to a faster machine. Hairy-chest machines, I call them. Sort of a pattern with my brother.

I went to the study and picked up that extension. "What's your password?" He paused before telling me, a hesitation that was justified because I snorted when he did. " *'BigTool'?*"

"I'm a mechanic."

"Oh, sure." I logged on and pulled down his e-mail. "Whoa, you get a lot of stuff. Mechanics must be chatty people."

"Look for something from JasperP, probably subject-headed '300S Coupe.' "

"Here it is." He made funny little noises as I read him what I thought was an indecipherable message. But it must have made sense to him, as he thanked me cheerfully.

"Good news?" I said.

"There's hope for the bedeviled car after all," he said. "I'll probably be late and then I'm going to Claire's. Do you have plans?"

"Nothing special."

"I'll be up early so I may not see you. I think I found the sled I want down in Minneapolis."

"Why Minneapolis? There's a shop on every county-road junction around here."

"Better selection, better prices. Besides, every dealer around here knows how I lost my old sled. I'm a little tired of the teasing."

"What do they say?"

"Stuff like, 'Just for you, Scotty, we'll throw in a wet suit.' It's irritating and it's distracting. I want to talk about the machines and they just want to joke."

Serious stuff, buying a power toy.

Serious and complicated, I guess. It took him four trips over three weeks. He had to shop around, haggle over price, order, select accessories and gear, and then—a red-letter day in my brother's life—he got to pick up the dream machine. Four trips and I wasn't invited along even once.

"I'll be home for supper," he said before he left on the great day. "It's Friday night. Let's kick off the weekend and have a real meal."

"A real meal that *I* cook?"

"I'll pick up some things. You could start a chicken after school."

"If it's a real meal, why don't we have company? You could invite Claire."

Not amused.

"Is she going to Minneapolis with you? When am I going to meet her?"

He blew off my questions the way he always blew off my interest in his girlfriend. Over the past few weeks I'd gotten bold and asked about her every chance I got. If he can be so mysterious about his love life, I can be obnoxious. I pushed him to exasperation once, which is how I finally learned her age: thirty-three. An older woman.

It made me wonder sometimes, was she pushing to learn about *me*?

I watched him pour coffee into a travel mug. Why not push as far as I dared? "Do you love her?" I asked.

He spilled hot coffee over his hand. Didn't swear,

didn't mutter a thing. Just rinsed his hand, dried it on a towel, started pouring again. I waited. I knew he'd heard me.

"No," he said finally. "I don't love her."

Scott spoke clearly and firmly, but later, when I was going over everything he ever said and did in those last days, I decided that there was something wrong about the way he had said it. He'd said "don't," but I think he meant "won't."

I let him get away without any more questions about his private life. I'd have loved to be going with him, but I hadn't been invited, had even been flatly refused when I begged. "You should study," he said. "Finals next week, right?"

Right, as always.

School *was* pressing down, and I had ArdenArt orders to finish. I loved my woodworking, but the business of it had become as tedious as school; filling orders for frames and mirrors based on old inspirations was a lot like doing homework. I'd much rather be working up new ideas, like the one I had gotten a few days before when I was in the c-store prowling through the cheap candy.

"Darn, I forgot," I muttered, and ran out of the house, waving my arms to stop him as he backed down the driveway.

He looked irritated as he rolled down the window. "What?"

"Remember that bulk candy store at the Rosedale Mall?"

"Yes. So?"

"I need wax lips."

. . .

"One box of wax lips, eighteen dollars and ninety-five cents."

"Did you get a receipt?"

"This is for ArdenArt?" He was stunned.

"Why else would I need them?"

"You're decorating frames with red lips?"

My poor, dull, dim-witted brother. "Of course not," I said patiently. "Makeup mirrors."

Minutes later he was on the phone telling Claire about the lips. He glowed, he laughed, he whispered, he twisted the cord around his wrist.

But no, he didn't love her.

We had our real supper. I'd come straight home from school and produced a nicely roasted chicken. He had brought interesting side dishes from an Italian deli in St. Paul. We both ate too much. A real supper.

After cleanup I went outside to admire the new snowmobile. I needed some coaxing because it was cold, one of the low days in a week of roller-coaster weather. I hugged myself and trotted in place on the fresh snow in the driveway. "Nice," I said, but I really couldn't share his pleasure. He saw fun and speed. I saw thin ice and black water.

"Al and I are going out tomorrow to break her in. What do you say afterwards we go out for dinner? There's that new steak place."

I was shocked. Saturday-night date with my brother? Since when? "Sorry, Scott, but I've made plans with Jean. School play. Unless you want to join us and go see Penokee High's production of *Macbeth*?"

He didn't, of course. I'm not sure I did, but it's a

small town, it was Saturday night, and I knew everyone in the cast. And, as it turned out, the play wasn't bad, though all the guys looked silly wearing fake facial hair.

Scott was home when I got in from the play, close to midnight. He was nursing a beer and listening to music. A woman vocalist, jazzy, unfamiliar. I foraged in the kitchen for my own bedtime snack. Toast.

I was slathering peanut butter on a third slice when he joined me. "What's that?" I asked.

He held up his beer bottle and looked at it. "Pig's Eye."

"No, the music."

"One of Mom's CDs. Ella Fitzgerald sings Cole Porter. Her favorite. It's her birthday today, you know."

"Ella Fitzgerald's? No, I didn't—"

"Mom's."

I finished a bite of toast. "I guess I'd forgotten." A small offense, brother. Don't look at me like that.

"Hers was February second and his was November twenty-eighth," he said.

"I know that. I just forgot. Sorry, okay?"

But he didn't want an apology, he wanted a promise. "Don't forget, Arden. What little you know about them, don't ever forget."

14

Years from now, when I reflect on my junior year in high school, I suspect that I will have no trouble deciding upon my greatest achievement. It will not be my solid A in biology. Not the money I'd made with ArdenArt. Not even the Thai curry I produced last fall for Scott's birthday.

It will be the pompadour.

Right before Thanksgiving I'd had an English assignment to write a personal essay based on a family photo. I found one of my parents taken on the day Mom graduated from medical school. She had this huge amount of hair piled on her head. Not sixties-beehive, but turn-of-the-century puffs. A pompadour.

Sometimes I forget what my parents looked like, and I had totally forgotten that my mother once had hair like mine. Long, thick, reddish brown.

The teacher wanted five to seven pages of familial insight, but I was more interested in the mysterious man standing behind my father in the picture. I wrote about the stranger, and it steamed the teacher. C plus. Okay, maybe I didn't produce a great essay. But after weeks of practice, I did manage to produce great hair. Special-occasion hair. Prom-night hair. Graduation-day hair.

But for the pomp's first public appearance, it was trip-to-the-mall hair.

"How do I look?" I asked Scott.

He poured some orange juice and drank before answering. "You look like a member of a very conservative religious group. And I'm not sure it works with the pants."

I frowned. New hair deserved new pants, so I'd purchased some red-and-green-plaid logger's pants. Thirty-three-fifty at the farm-supply store.

"If you're going to criticize, then at least let me have

that bagel. I'm running late and Kady and Jean will be here any minute." He handed it over. "Funny smell," I said as I lifted it to my mouth. I bit down anyway.

"Just oiled my jacket; maybe there was a little left on my hands."

He had his new snowmobiling jacket on his lap. Black leather, silver studs. Scott stuck a hand into a sleeve and pulled out what looked like a Day-Glo–green jump rope, only this rope would never be approved for children: short, sharp metal claws protruded from the handles.

"Quite a weapon," I said. I took another bite of bagel and tongued it into the side of my mouth. "Expecting trouble on the trail?"

"Don't talk with your mouth full. It's an ice claw. A tool, not a weapon."

"What's it for?"

"Some guys wear one through their coat sleeves; then if you break through and land in water, you've got it handy for holding on to the ice." He jabbed the air with one end of the rope.

"Sort of like mitten strings on a baby's coat?" I picked up the other end and ran my thumb over the sharp metal teeth. "Yes, a perfect infant accessory."

"Thanks for the image; I guess I'll keep mine in the saddlebag." He yanked it and the rope flew out of my hand and scraped across the smooth leather of his jacket sleeve, scratching the newly oiled surface.

He swore. I smiled and grabbed my own jacket. "Don't miss and hit yourself, brother. That looks like a twenty-stitch weapon."

He held both ends and jabbed the air again—left; right. "Just stab the ice and pull myself out of the water," he said. "Oh, Arden, I'm taking tomorrow off. Leave the Honda home, and I'll change the oil."

A car horn honked.

"Gotta go. Don't look for me for supper, okay?"

He nodded, intent on his ice claws. Left, right; left, right. "I might be eating at Claire's."

"Should I wait up?"

He made a face and faked a jab at me; then his hand froze midswipe as if he had clawed a thought out of thin air. "That hair is actually very nice."

"Thank you. Gotta go."

"Mom used to wear it that way. Gosh, you really look like her. I've never noticed it before. It's almost weird, what a difference that hairstyle makes. You look a *lot* like her, Arden."

"Where are my gloves? Did you move them last night? Did you clean up? I told you I would."

"She cut it, though. Right before you were born. Short, real short."

"I've seen pictures." Car horn again. Where were the darn gloves?

"I remember the night she did it. She had friends over to the apartment, back when we were living in Milwaukee. She was huge with you, and there were all these women sitting around talking."

"Tell me later."

He grabbed my arm, dropping the rope. As it fell, a claw snagged on my fleece sleeve. "Arden, wait, listen to this."

"I'm late, Scott." I picked off the claw. "This is really wicked."

"It was the night she came up with your name. You know how she got it? She—"

"You picked a bad time to tell me a story, brother." I walked to the front door and he followed. I opened the door and winced at the blast of cold air. "I'm late, it looks like snow, we've got a long drive, I'll see you later."

"Arden—"

"*What?*" I snapped. The look in his eyes grabbed me. It was as if he were searching for something. Maybe for the memory of her.

Scott smiled. "Have a great day, Arden. And watch out for flying bowling pins."

That was not an idle warning. Twice before, when I'd assisted the twins, I had been slightly wounded by flying objects. Sometimes when they wanted to make a quick change in the show, they'd toss things to whoever they'd corralled to assist. I was one of the usual suspects. The two times I'd gotten hit, I had looked away at the wrong moment, perhaps enchanted by the sight of some young child in their audience adjusting underwear or picking a nose.

"What are these?" Kady said. She leaned over the car seat and fingered my pants.

"Farm-store special. You might say something nice about the hair."

I could see Jean eyeing me in the rearview mirror. "We could, if you wanted to hear a lie."

Kady shook her head. "Arden, you're going to scare the little kids."

Jean put the car in gear and we raced in reverse down the driveway. "Five dollars says that hair doesn't last the day. It's already sagging." She shifted again and we lurched forward.

I groped in the seat cracks for the seat belt, pulled it free, and wiped away the food bits that had popped out. I buckled, then stretched to see myself in the mirror. God, I looked good. I patted my hair. "Five dollars says it does."

I won the bet. Maybe it wasn't an entirely fair victory because I repinned once during the show, when they were intent on exchanging balloons loaded with ketchup. But it was a fair repin, I argued with myself, because they had just publicly coerced me into joining the performance, hauling me up to hold balloons as they filled them. Both of them had made a big deal of rolling their eyes, smirking, and pointing at me whenever one of the plastic ketchup bottles they were squeezing emitted a fartlike noise. The crowd of children roared, loving the clowning, the noise, my dismay.

As soon as they were tossing the mushy balloons, I sat and defiantly repinned my hair. Dignity was gone, but the five dollars *would* be mine.

The hair lasted through the show and through the

crush of autograph-seeking children who besieged us during our late lunch in the food court. It even survived trying on clothes at Ragstock, where I insisted we go after the mall. I'd seen an ad for a new shipment of bowling shirts. Wasn't much of a shipment, as it turned out, and there weren't any as nice as my "Franz" or "Morrie," but there was a whole rack of Japanese baseball team shirts. Who could resist?

I tried on seven and bought one. Gold and purple, with plenty of Japanese script on the sleeve and the name ARITA across the front.

"Does it look good with the pants?" I said to Kady when I stepped out of the dressing room. She cupped her ear. Music was blasting out of the store's speakers. I shrugged and returned to the cubicle. Okay, maybe the colors didn't work with the green-and-red-plaid pants, but it felt good, and that's all that should matter.

The hair lasted through Jean's slow perusal of true-crime fiction at the used-book store, and through Kady's detailed discussion of college application essays with a guy at the coffee shop. I was about to refill my cup from the pump pots when I realized what they were doing: stretching out the day in a gambit to win the bet.

"I need to get going," I whispered to Jean. "I'm not feeling so good." I could gambit myself. I put my hand on my stomach.

She looked a little worried. Would I vomit in their car? "Let's go," she replied.

A good thing that we did, because by the time we left downtown Duluth and were on the long bridge that crossed the harbor to Wisconsin, snow was falling. At first it was just nonthreatening fluffy stuff, but ten miles out of Superior we hit a serious storm. Wind and snow mixed to obscure the road; Jean slowed the car to a crawl. Kady changed music on the tape player and Beck's raucous vocals gave way to soothing Mozart piano sonatas.

The wind eased a bit as we turned onto our street. Jean picked up speed and drove too fast into their driveway, and the car skidded to a stop just inches from the garage door.

I patted my hair. "It lasted the day. I win."

"Maybe so," Jean said. "But who got you home safe?"

Good point. And I had cheated, slightly. I tipped my head in concession, pins dropped, and the hair toppled down.

16

Scott wasn't home, no surprise. Probably cozily dining with the girlfriend. I checked the machine for messages, then made a face when I saw that he hadn't left it on. What had I missed? What wild and exciting event in this town had I missed hearing about?

I decided to count on a snow day tomorrow and skipped doing homework. Nothing was due anyway, so why strain myself? I did have several ArdenArt orders due, so I went to the workshop. Nothing was working, though. I finished one wax-lip mirror, but I nearly supplied it with the real thing when I slipped off my stool and almost sliced my face with a mat knife. Then I spilled my cache of precious lips on the floor and hit my head on the worktable as I rose from collecting them. "Give it up, girl," I ordered myself.

Nine-thirty. The day was dying, but I still had choices. TV, bathtub, bed, or a book? I picked all four.

I was in Scott's huge tub when I heard the phone ring. Had I turned on the machine? No, I remembered as it rang for the fifth time. Six, seven. "Let it go," I said as I lowered myself in the water.

I was walking with Jane Eyre across the moors when it rang again. I slapped the book closed, swung my feet out of bed, tripped on the bedding, stubbed my toe on the doorjamb, and was hobbling when I reached the phone. It stopped. I dialed the Drummonds' number. "Did you call?" I asked Jean. "Someone called."

"Not us. Think we'll have school tomorrow?"

I looked out the window. "It's letting up."

Jean groaned. "I was counting on a snow day. I didn't study for history."

"I blew off a paper. Thank God for first-hour study halls."

"Maybe it'll pick up again."

"We can hope. Call me if you hear."

I'd never spent a night by myself. Sure, plenty of nights I'd been alone until late, but never the whole night, not all the way through. What with the wind-borne noises it might have bothered me this time, except I didn't *know* I'd be alone all night. I went to bed assuming that my dear, reliable brother would roar home during the wee hours and, as usual, be up in time to have juice made for me in the morning.

I went without juice. I would have gone without breakfast, too, except that Mr. Drummond was taking muffins to work and I cadged one from the bag as soon as I got in their car. Determined to believe we'd have the day off, I hadn't set my alarm and was rudely awakened at seven-thirty, when Jean called to offer a ride with her father. "You haven't shoveled your driveway," she said. "The plow came by and you'll never get out. Might as well come with us. We leave in five minutes."

I can be dressed in five minutes. Sweater, jeans, socks, and boots—hell, I can be dressed in three. Maybe I can't produce a pompadour in that time, but I can be clean and combed. I cannot be cheerful, though. That's a slow process; don't rush me.

"Hey," I greeted the Drummonds when I opened the car door. I knocked snow off my boots before getting in. It had drifted deeply on the front walk and I had kicked my way through.

"Late start for you and Scott?" Mr. Drummond asked. "Or is he taking the day off?" That was the first I realized I hadn't seen a sign of my brother. Of course, with my sleep-induced grogginess, there could have been a troop of naked fencers in the kitchen and I wouldn't have noticed. I looked back at the untouched snow on the driveway and the empty spot where he usually parked his sled.

You dog, you, I thought. So he spent the night with the girlfriend. That's a first. Must be serious.

Mr. Drummond smiled at me in the mirror, waiting for an answer.

"Day off," I said. True, and all he needed to know.

. . .

The snow on the driveway was still untouched when I returned on the bus after school. Only the letter carrier's tracks crossed over mine on the front walk. I took the mail out of the box and let myself into the house. I went right to the phone, sure he'd called and left a message. I was curious about his excuse: the storm was bad, it got late, I'd had a few beers, none of your business. All true, take your pick.

There was only one message, logged at 2:30 P.M. I punched the button and played the tape:

Hello to the Munros. Scott, this is Claire. Sorry we got signals crossed about dinner last night. Wish you had made it. Oh, the car wasn't making that noise this morning, but I still think it should be checked. Can you get it in this week? That's all. Um, hi, Arden, if that's who answers.

I walked to his bedroom and pushed open the door. The bed was neatly made, a shirt and sweater were draped on a chair—the same shirt and sweater that had been there last night. The same mess of baseball cards and comic books on his dresser.

"Scott?" I called. My voice sounded loud, sharp, tight.

I checked the bathroom. The towel I'd used was the top item in the hamper. The toilet seat was down. My socks lay on the floor.

He hadn't been home. He'd never been to his girlfriend's.

His truck was in the garage, his driving gloves on the kitchen counter.

I looked at the back door. "Walk in," I whispered. "Walk in now."

The phone book had a Poole, C. listed with a rural address: County Road PN. Where the hell was PN?

The message on her machine was my second major shock of the day: a child's voice. *This is Hannah. Mom and I can't get to the phone, but leave a message. Thanks.*

Mom and I?

Oh brother, brother. No wonder you didn't spend nights there. I left my own message, hoping I'd disguised my surprise.

This is Arden Munro, Scott's sister. Please call me. Thanks.

I poured a soda and wondered, should I be worried? Didn't matter, I *was* worried.

I called the police station and asked for Al. When in doubt, call a cop.

"We'll have him call you," the lady said.

Al rang in five minutes. I could hear restaurant noise in the background and resisted making a doughnut joke. I told him why I was calling. He wasn't too concerned and told me to check with Claire.

"No," I answered firmly. "He never went there. Claire called and left a message. She was kind of wondering where he'd been last night, only she didn't come out and say it. But you could tell."

"His sled is gone?"

"That's what I said, Al. The 'Cuda and his truck are both here, his sled is gone, and he didn't make it to where he said he was going last night."

"Let me make some calls. And stay there; I'm coming over."

Cop on the way—a bad sign.

The heat hadn't been turned up all day; Scott always did that. I felt cold, so cold. I crossed my arms and looked out the window.

Winter dark settles in about four o'clock and it comes quickly, a sneak attack after a day of blinding sun-on-snow. Across the street, the Drummonds' lights went on through the house like a current—flick, flick, flick. I saw Kady in the suddenly illuminated kitchen working at the counter, saw her mother walk past behind her, saw Jean pull the curtains in her room, saw their father pushing a vacuum in the living room.

Had anyone looked at this house, they'd observe nothing but stillness and shadows.

17

"This is what we know," Al said as soon as he walked in the door. "Scott was at Winker's Tavern around four yesterday afternoon. He told the men there that he'd been out alone and was headed to Claire's place. She's the naturalist at the state park. That's where she lives."

County Road PN, I thought.

He reported more. Scott and the others at Winker's had discussed the distance to the park. Eight miles, they'd decided, if you went on the county trail and then up the road. Six if you crossed the river and rode the state trail. Scott had been drinking a little. Buck, the bartender, thought maybe three beers. And he'd been giving advice on cars, made a promise to check out Tom Koski's Lumina in exchange for a load of firewood.

He'd made a toast to his girlfriend, though by then no one was left to hear except Buck.

Buck had been in the back when he left, and he thought maybe he heard him head down toward the river. Hard to tell, he was rattling glasses, cleaning up.

"That's all?" I said.

"I called Claire. She'd just gotten home and heard your message. She confirmed that she never saw him yesterday, hadn't talked to him since he and I were out there on Saturday." He made two fists and rubbed them on his thighs. "The sheriff has called a search."

"At night?"

"They can start by patrolling the trails around that area. It will be morning by the time a whole crew gets there. He's called for the State Patrol helicopter. It uses an infrared system and can spot bodies in the woods."

Bodies. We both flinched when he said it. "I want to come with you. I want to help, Al." I picked up a pillow and punched it. "I should have figured out yesterday that something was wrong. I should have called you then. It's been a whole day, Al, he's been out there for a day."

"You didn't know. Claire didn't know. Everyone thought he was somewhere else. No one knew he was missing. Arden, there are two shelters on those trails. Maybe he had trouble and holed up for the night. We're checking now."

"I want to help."

"Arden, if we don't find him on the trail tonight, the search gets tough. You've never even been on a sled."

"I'm telling you, I want to help."

He took a moment to speak. "If we don't find him tonight, it's not good. If we find him, you don't want to be there. Not when we're looking for a— Cripes, Arden, is there someone who can stay with you tonight? Maybe those two girls, Danny Drummond's sisters, the twins."

He couldn't come out and say it, but this is what he meant: We're not looking for your brother, we're looking for a body.

Al called the Drummonds and within five minutes Kady and her mom were over with food. I didn't eat. They talked to Al and got the story while I looked out the window. Mr. Drummond arrived with his snowblower. He went to work on our driveway, disappearing behind a soaring shaft of powder.

Al left and called an hour later with bad news. The trail and the river had been patrolled, with no sign of Scott.

"This damn wind," Mrs. Drummond said. "They won't know where to look, it's blown away any tracks. Goddamn wind. Goddamn it to hell."

Kady stared at her mother, who never swore.

Midnight. Kady was asleep in a chair, Mrs. Drummond was knitting. I sat and stared out the window, holding a cup of cold tea.

Two A.M. Mrs. Drummond snored softly, Kady talked in her sleep. "Huh-ya, huh-ya, huh-ya," their juggling chant.

Four A.M. I moved my tea mug to the other hand.

At six I was in my car. As I backed down the driveway I looked at the house and saw Mrs. Drummond in the window. She lifted a hand and waved.

Winker's Tavern was crowded, but no one was drinking beer. I had to park out on the county road because the lot was full. Two sheriff's cars, a State Patrol cruiser, lots of pickups. A German shepherd was tethered outside the door. It rose and stared as I approached. I kicked snow off my shoes and pushed open the tavern door. The buzz of conversation had been so loud I'd heard it through the door, but as soon as I walked in, dead silence.

"Geez, Arden," Al said. "Everyone, this is Scott's sister." People crowded around, touching my arm, tugging my sleeves, laying hands on my shoulders, talking. I heard only snippets and kept jerking my head back and forth, trying to respond to each with a nod or a smile.

. . . snow cover on the river . . .

. . . if I'd known he was alone . . .

. . . river ice . . .

. . . search and rescue . . .

. . . river current . . .

The river, the river, the river. On and on, people kept talking about the river.

"I want to go out," I said, and they all shut up.

"Arden," Al replied, "you don't even have boots." Everyone looked at my feet.

True, no boots. I sagged, and someone put an arm around me. "I want to know what you're doing," I said to everyone. "Don't hide it from me."

A big guy came over and introduced himself, Buck

Winker. "How 'bout some eggs?" he said. I nodded and let myself be led to a booth. Someone brought me cocoa. I warmed my hands. Just the walk from the car had chilled me through. Twenty below windchill, Buck said when he delivered the eggs.

A woman wearing deputy brown slid into the booth. "Felicity Kay. I'm the search coordinator. We've got twenty people out, Arden. They're doing a systematic search of the area. The patrol helicopter should arrive soon. We'll have it do a flyover of the river, and then we'll pull in the people and let it cover the woods."

I peppered my eggs.

"I've led a lot of searches, Arden. I know you want to help. And you can."

I set down the pepper shaker. "Stay out of the way?"

"If you don't want to wait at home, and I can certainly understand that, then just stay here. Buck will take care of you."

I looked at Buck, who stood behind the bar, a wooden toothpick rolling across his lips. He winked. Felicity Kay rose and zipped up her coat. In spite of the panic that was gripping me, I had to smile—she even zipped with authority.

There's maybe no sound louder than a helicopter, and the one that buzzed the bar at that moment nearly knocked me out of the booth and rocked glasses off the shelves. Buck cocked his head and looked up. Deputy Kay turned and strode out of the building.

In a moment it was just Buck and me in the tavern. "Good eggs," I said.

He leaned on his arms on the bar. "Scotty started coming here this winter and we all liked him real well,

Arden. Kind of a greenhorn, considering he'd lived in Penokee for a while."

Twelve years, I thought, if you count the year at Yale.

"Never even hunted, he told me."

"Didn't fish, either," I said.

"Not like most of the guys, that's for sure. But we liked him. He was funny, sheesh. Always had one to make you laugh. And sure, maybe he didn't know the first thing about what was around him once he stepped outside, but the guy could work his way through an engine." Buck stood erect and stretched. "I'll be in the back doctoring numbers for the taxman. Just yell if you want anything."

I poked at my eggs, then smashed what remained under the tines of the fork.

Okay, so I'd always gotten lousy grades in English, but I was alert enough to have learned one thing: past tense. I knew what that was and why you used it.

Past tense. Buck had used it to talk about my brother.

I fell asleep in a bar. I realize that for most people this would not be an event you'd want to talk about. After I ate my eggs and finished my cocoa, I stretched my legs out on the booth's bench, covered myself with my coat, and prepared to spend the morning watching the entrance of the tavern. But I slept.

Drool dripping across my chin woke me up. Or maybe it was the yelping dog. Or the sound of car doors slamming. Or maybe I'd just had enough rest. I woke up hurting, my neck stiff and my butt sore from the hard wood. I knew then I'd never make a good drunk and I smiled, thinking that Scott would be pleased.

My smile passed fast. Scott was why I'd been sleeping here, and Scott was gone. For a moment I'd forgotten.

Three men sat at the bar. When they heard me stir, they turned around to look, glanced at each other, then put on their hats and rose to leave.

Buck appeared with fresh cocoa. "Deputy wants to talk with you. She's outside. I'll get her."

I wanted him to take his time. Had to be bad news; anything else, they wouldn't have let me sleep.

I got up and walked to the window. People were tossing things into trucks, two men were shaking hands, a woman was on her knees stroking the dog. Deputy Kay was talking with a state trooper. She turned, spotted me in the window, and started walking.

The ends of a bright-green rope swung from her hand. A green rope with metal teeth. My brother's ice claws. Something clawed at my throat. I met her at the door and reached for the rope. "That's his," I said. "Where did you find it?"

Al was right behind her and he took my arm. "Let's sit down."

"Where did you find it?"

"Someone was patrolling the riverbanks and spotted this just beyond the bridge channel. We blew up the inflatable walkway and recovered it. One end was secured in ice at the edge of open water. Can you identify this as your brother's?"

"I told you already, yes, it was his. It was new. He was showing it to me this morning. I mean Sunday morning. I teased him, I warned him it would be like a baby's mitten string if he wore it through his jacket. He got pissed and said he wouldn't wear it."

"Arden, I've called in the air and ground searchers."

"Why?"

"We did some dragging from the walkway and recovered a helmet and saddlebag. His wallet and a few other things were in it."

"He could have gotten out of the water. You said the claw was secured in ice. He must have pulled himself out. He could be walking in the woods. People get disoriented. You can't stop looking for him."

"We haven't stopped, but it's been two days, Arden, and now we have proof he was wet. Even if he got out of the water, he's had two nights of subzero temperatures."

Say it, Deputy. Say it, say it, say it. "You think he's dead?"

Al sat down in a booth and put his head in his hands.

"We're focusing on the river now. I've called for divers."

Say the bad words, Deputy. I can. "Now you're looking for a body."

She dropped the rope on a table. Melting ice slid off the wood handle. "Please let someone take you home."

Al rose and zipped his jacket. "C'mon, Arden. I'll drive."

"No."

Deputy Kay exhaled impatiently. "You don't want to see what they're going to find, Arden; a drowned body is a nightmare."

"I have to," I said. "Otherwise I'll imagine far worse."

"No," Al whispered. "There is nothing worse."

He took me to the Drummonds', where Mrs. D. was waiting at the door. Kady and Jean had stayed home from school and they hovered silently behind her. She stepped forward to hug me, but I turned aside and laid my coat on a chair, deflecting her gesture. "They haven't found him yet," I said, "but they're pretty sure they know where he is. Jean, okay if I go lie down in your room?"

Al and Mrs. D. looked at each other. Obviously they had anticipated tears or some sort of grieving fit.

I sat at Jean's desk and sketched on the back of old school papers. Drew trees. A river. I played mental games and concocted scenarios. I tried to figure ways he could be alive. Even after getting wet. Even after two nights.

Two nights. I pounded the desk and a pile of small rubber balls bounced and scattered. Why hadn't I wondered where he was? Why hadn't his stupid girlfriend kept calling so she could yell at him for not showing up?

She had, of course. I remembered the phone ringing persistently while I was in the bath that night, then again when I was reading. Why hadn't he left the machine on? Why hadn't I turned it on? She'd have left a message, I would have listened to it, I would have worried. We could have found him.

I heard the phone ringing and was in the kitchen by the third ring. Kady started to say something but I waved her off. Al was taking the message, nodding grimly, rubbing his hand over his eyes.

"What?" I said as soon as he'd hung up.

"A diver found his sled in the water, downriver a bit from where they found the rope."

"Did they find Scott?"

He shook his head. "The deputy sheriff has called off the search. The sled was in a deep spot with strong current, north of the bridge." Al closed his eyes. "It never freezes solidly by that bridge, no matter how cold. The water is channeled too narrowly, the current is too strong." He looked at me. "On Saturday Scotty and I took some runs over open patches on Minnow Lake. He was blowing over them like a circuit pro. But a river is different. The rim ice is weaker. It can look safe, but it never is. He didn't know."

"They called off the search? They're going to leave him there?" I was standing inches away from him, looking straight up at his distress.

"She can't keep divers in that water."

"Just *leave* him in the river?"

He looked around, he couldn't look right at me. "Arden, they can't do a systematic search. Not in that cold water. Not in that spot. She can't risk divers for a body retrieval. The river is too dangerous."

I pounded on his chest. He bit his lip and swayed, taking it. "Well, that's obvious, isn't it?" I shouted.

My anger charged Mrs. Drummond into action. She

held out a hand and murmured something to ease me. Al was near tears. Kady and Jean both stepped toward me.

I stepped back. "Don't touch me."

They all froze.

"Don't try to help me."

Mrs. Drummond crossed her arms. Al's tears slid out.

"Just everybody go away."

Within hours the entire population of Penokee kicked into funeral mode, and for over a week people, food, and flowers poured into the Drummonds' house. I stayed holed up in Jean's room, coming out whenever a new visitor was announced and retreating as soon as I could. Everybody was nice, maybe too nice. I shook hands and shook heads with parents of friends, teachers, Scott's coworkers, neighbors, and classmates. Jace Dailey, the first guy I ever kissed, drove all the way from the town in Minnesota where his family had moved after freshman year, and I kissed him again.

Jace didn't know what to say, which was a pretty honest reaction. I welcomed it, as I'd gotten really tired of the people who rushed toward me with soothing words and murmurs of comforting nonsense. Not Jace. After the kiss we looked at each other, then glanced around at all the people looking at us. Then he spoke: "It's pretty shitty," he said in a low voice.

Had to laugh at that. And agree. "Yeah."

Jace stuffed his hands in his jeans. "I remember once when I walked you home from a party at Dawn's . . . Hey, she moved away, didn't she? That's what I heard."

"St. Paul."

"She like it?"

"No one hears from her."

"Too bad, she was fun. Anyway, I'd walked home with you that time and I swear within a minute he was out the door and ready to talk. I had my new bike and he wanted to talk about trail riding and stuff. Couldn't believe it. Just like that—bang! Big brother jumps in, making sure nothing happens. He really watched over you, didn't he?"

That did it. Sweet old Jace with the memory of Scott preempting his make-out moves did it. Tears I'd been sucking back for days let loose.

"Geez, Arden," Jace said. "I'm sorry. Man, how stupid, I'm always saying the wrong thing. Maybe I shouldn't have come. I was in town seeing my grandma and I heard about it and I felt awful. I'm sorry."

I stood there dumbly, soaking my face while he looked about for help. People started pushing tissues at me. Kady appeared and grabbed my arm. "Let's go to my room."

I jerked my arm away. "Why? This is what everyone came for, isn't it? To look at the grieving survivor?"

My nose was running at the same pace as my tears and I wiped with a sleeve. Damn, it was my new red wool sweater, dry clean only.

Time of crisis, funny what you think of.

. . .

My fit worked. The extra people left, except for Jace. When I finally sobered up, my face was a mess, something Jean and Jace were happy to point out.

"Kind of splotchy," Jace said.

"Pretty swollen," Jean added.

"Get lost," I said, and sat down between them on the davenport.

"When's the funeral?" Jace said.

Beat, beat, beat—you could almost hear the hearts speed up in the room.

"That," Kady said tersely, "is the second bonehead thing you've said today."

Jace looked confused; the effect was sweet.

"No funeral," I said. "No body, no funeral."

Mrs. Drummond sat down, and a dish towel dropped to her lap. "Oh, Arden, people will want something. A memorial service. It's good to say good-bye. And perhaps we could write up something for the paper."

"You mean an obituary. No. Then I'd just have to do it again when they do find him."

Kady and Mrs. Drummond looked at each other, then rose from their chairs and went to the kitchen.

"I think that's smart," said Jean. "Why torture yourself twice?" She stood up and dusted crumbs off her lap onto the floor. "Gotta go study. Physics test tomorrow."

Jace rose, too. "Me too, I mean, I've gotta go too, and pick up my mom at my grandma's, then we've got a ways home."

A lot of people had done a lot of nice things for me in the past few days. But his visit after three years away was maybe the nicest. Time for the third kiss?

He thought so. Then, "I'll call," he said.

"Good," I answered.

Jean didn't go study until we heard Jace's car drive away. She crossed her arms and tried to be stern. "Of all the stupid things you have done since I've known you, this may be tops."

"What do you mean?"

"Hitching yourself to a guy who lives hours away."

"I haven't hitched myself to anyone. Don't be silly. He was just making a condolence call."

She smirked. "And I'd say you looked pretty condoled, especially when he had his mouth on yours."

I started to protest, then stopped. It had felt good.

Mrs. Drummond called from the kitchen, "Veggie burgers or spaghetti?" Kady chimed in, "Vote now or no complaining later!"

Jean tipped her head and lowered her voice. "Isn't life with the two happy homemakers driving you crazy?"

"It's not that bad, and it is nice to have someone else taking care of things. They do kind of flutter around, but I mostly ignore it."

She nodded. "Me too, but it took me eighteen years to learn how. You might find it tougher to ignore them once you've moved in for good and things are settled."

"What?"

Her mouth opened and closed twice, a popping circle of pink. "That's what everyone's been saying. My parents were picked as guardians years ago. Scott did that. You're supposed to live with us."

"No, I won't."

Kady and her mother had come to the kitchen door and were listening.

Jean held up a hand. "I know you knew. We used to joke about it."

"Joke, yes. I'm not staying." I turned to Mrs. D. "I can't live here, not forever."

Mrs. Drummond fluttered her hand. "We'll have to talk, Arden. Maybe not tonight, but there are things to go over."

"We don't have to talk. There's no argument. I can't leave my house, my workshop. I have a home."

Kady leaned a hip against the doorjamb. "You won't want to be alone. That's crazy. You can't."

"I do want to be alone and I want to be alone now. I'm leaving." Coat, boots, things from the bathroom. I had an armload of belongings and didn't bother to close the door behind me. I trudged through the snow, head down against the wind, orphan in a storm.

It was good to have my own bed, own bathroom, own mess. For the first time in days I felt like I could think straight, felt like eating, felt like laughing at Letterman's jokes.

Too bad I couldn't sleep. I hadn't slept much at all since my nap in the bar, the day of the search. I was tired enough, but there was an impediment: vivid and vicious nightmares. They'd begun the first night after the searchers found the sled. The dreams were all the same. Fish and my brother. It had reached the point where I couldn't even close my eyes in daytime without seeing the same underwater scene: Scott undulating like seaweed while fish poked and prodded him. Big ones, little ones, nipping, biting. I usually woke up when the biggest fish turned around in my mind-screen and swam toward me, mouth gasping, gills pulsing, soulless dead eyes pinpointed on my fear.

The worst night I had was that first one back in my own house, though I'd never tell Mrs. D. That was the night I stayed asleep long enough to see the fish nibble him down to a rack of bones that rolled off one by one in the current. Knowing what was in store, I preferred not to sleep. So when I opened my door to company a few days after leaving the Drummonds', I looked awful and felt worse. Of course, it wasn't a social call, which didn't help my mood.

There were five of them: Mr. and Mrs. Drummond; Al; Mrs. Rutledge, the school counselor; and John Abrahms, our family lawyer. They'd arrived together, walking across the street from the Drummonds' as a group. The orphan committee.

They sat and faced me in the living room, sort of the way I'd always imagined a drug intervention would go. There was a girl at school who'd been through that. All these people came and confronted her, forcing her to admit she was chemically dependent and spiraling down the drain. We love you, so we'll stay and harass you until you admit you're screwing up your life.

That's what this was, a life intervention.

I let Mrs. Rutledge hug me, and I nodded to John. He was another of Scott's buddies. He'd helped me with ArdenArt legalities and he took care of the taxes. "Sign here, Arden"—that was our relationship. I folded my hands. I'd sign nothing tonight.

Obviously they'd brought Mrs. Rutledge to be the mouth. I'd known her all my school life. She'd been my first- and third-grade teacher; then she'd gone to the middle school as counselor when I went to sixth grade; then she went to the high school just as I entered ninth grade. "The heart of the town has gone out to you," she said as an opener when we were all seated.

I made a face. The most recent nightmare had focused on that particular organ of my brother's.

She held her hands up. "You're right, sentiment isn't what we're here for."

She went on, talking about the people who cared about my future, how my brother had cared, why he'd made arrangements. She gave John his shot. He synopsized the will Scott had written years ago, slowing down to explain the guardianship. Then he talked about money—where it was, how much I had, what would be available, what would be tied up while settling the estate.

"Financially," he said cheerfully, "you're just fine."

With sleep-droopy eyes, I faced him. His smile died as he read my mind: Otherwise, I'm in the dump.

Mrs. Rutledge started another speech, and I halted her with my hand. "What has to happen for me to be alone, legally?"

"An application for emancipation," said John. "A judge would rule."

"That's what I want."

"You can't be alone—"

"I *am* alone," I snapped. "My parents died in a jungle and my brother is at the bottom of a river and I am in this house and I am alone." I turned to the Drummonds. "This isn't against you, Mr. and Mrs. D."

Mr. Drummond tapped his fingers on his knee. "Clear enough to me, Arden. You've lost your parents, you've just lost your brother, and now you want to keep your home."

"Exactly. Thank you." John frowned. Mrs. Rutledge folded her hands. "Can't I even try to make it on my own?"

They all looked at each other, except for Al, who was staring at his feet, the position he'd been in all night. I wasn't sure why they'd brought him. Maybe to reinforce Scott's wishes, to be the best friend who knew what the deceased really wanted.

He raised his head and looked straight at me. "Scott was hoping you'd get to art school, see the world," he said. "He hoped you would do all the things he didn't do."

Yes, I'd guessed right.

"So for his sake, if they let you have your way, don't fuck up."

Mrs. Drummond inhaled sharply, her husband crossed his legs, John glanced at Mrs. Drummond, embarrassed for her. Mrs. Rutledge, a veteran school counselor used to a wide vocabulary, nodded.

"Any application for emancipation would be subject to evaluation," she said, "and we'd all have input. You'd have to show you were taking responsibility for yourself."

"In other words, you'd be watching."

"For your own good."

"We may as well give her a chance," Al said. His sharp tone caught my attention and made me wonder if he too was wrestling with dreams. I thought back to all the summer nights when he and Scott worked on the 'Cuda in the garage, laughing, putting away a few beers. More than once I'd heard Al coaxing Scott to get a snowmobile, making slightly dirty jokes about the thrill of the ride between his legs. Maybe he was blaming himself.

"If she wants to be alone so bad," Al said, "let her try it. Geez, she'll be eighteen in a year anyway."

They all murmured, Good point, yes, yes.

Mrs. Rutledge looked around. "Trial period of a month, shall we say?"

"A *month?*" I screeched. I wouldn't have the house cleaned in a month.

"End of the school year," said Mr. Drummond.

John tidied up the stack of papers, tapping them sharply against the briefcase. "Unless there's even the slightest indication that we need to step in earlier." They all turned to me grimly.

"Then," said Mrs. Drummond, "we tie the purse strings"—John nodded—"and get tough."

For my own good.

"I need to think," I said, and stood up. "Why don't we call it quits for now? Would anyone like something to eat? There's lots."

They all rose, John dropping papers off his lap. "Will you come into the office and sign things?" he said. "We need to get the names straight on the accounts, figure out some sort of an allowance. And would it be okay if

I took a look at Scott's desk and the computer? I need to make sure I have all the financial records."

I shrugged. "Help yourself."

"There's one more thing."

I massaged my forehead. Stop it, stop it, stop it.

"Walt Lorenzo told me to tell you that he'll need Scott's truck back."

I looked at him. They're hammering at my life and he wants to talk about the truck?

"It was leased on an employee program. Fortunately, the Honda is yours, right?"

I nodded as they all started discussing other things: the will, bank accounts, mutual funds, cars, insurance, our lawn service.

John saw that I wasn't tracking. "It never fails to make me feel like a goon, but I always have to tell clients that death uncovers a lot of details."

They all murmured, Yes, yes, so many things.

Details. That moment I felt more alone than ever. I was swimming in a nightmare while everyone else had moved on to details.

While John searched the study and Scott's room for financial records, Mrs. Rutledge, Al, and Mrs. D. moved on to the kitchen for tea. Mr. Drummond followed, then paused in the doorway. "She brought you some manicotti," he said. "She'll probably start making double batches of everything."

"I don't need it."

"She needs to do it. Arden, it's not very far to our house," he said, "but I know it could be the longest walk you ever make."

"I'll be fine."

"I think you will be. But if there's ever a time you don't feel fine, even if it's just for one bad night, you come on over. Open door, Arden."

It was Saturday, and he hadn't shaved. There was a dark grainy stubble on his chin, probably scratchy and rough to the touch. Had my father ever not shaved on the weekend? Had he ever worn baggy sweaters and paint-stained jeans? Did my mother hum when she worked in the kitchen? Did we ever eat manicotti?

I'd never know, would I? All the answers to all the questions had disappeared through thin ice.

21

There was enough manicotti for a dozen orphans. I'd never eat it, especially as about all I had eaten since I'd moved home was saltines and peanut butter. Penokee was still in funeral mode and people kept bringing things, so I had plenty of fancy cookies and elaborate hot dishes and bright gelatin salads. Absolutely no one brought me saltines and peanut butter.

I pulled the tray with the pasta tubes off a refrigerator shelf and held it until the cold metal numbed my hand. Then I put it back and reached for the milk. I opened the cardboard spout and a sour smell floated up.

A responsible person, I decided, does not drink sour milk. I'd have to remember this, in case the orphan committee made another visit and checked my refrigerator.

The parking lot of Penokee's only grocery store was packed. No way was I going to wind my way through the crush of people who were shopping because there was nothing else to do on a Saturday afternoon. I drove on to the nearest c-store.

I was leaning into the cooler, trying to rearrange milk cartons and get one of the freshest ones from the back, when I sensed someone behind me. I clamped down on a quart of skim and backed up.

When I straightened and turned, I was facing a beautiful woman. A sad, beautiful woman. I'd seen her once before, at my party.

"Arden?"

I'd had my head in the cooler and my butt in the air, but my brother's girlfriend had recognized me. "Claire?"

She nodded, then looked behind her. A small girl peeked out. "This is Hannah." She leaned over and whispered in her daughter's ear. The girl and I exchanged stares.

I cradled my milk carton. "I was kind of wondering if I'd ever meet you."

"I should have come by. I . . . wasn't up to it. I sent flowers."

"They were nice. Azaleas. Thanks." Suddenly I flashed on another responsibility: thank-you notes, something the orphan committee would certainly be checking. All that food, all those flowers—gawd, I'd be writing notes for weeks.

Claire reached behind her back and patted Hannah. The girl—five, six, how do you tell?—took a giant sideways step and faced me. "That's bad about Scott," she said before hiding again behind her mother.

The doorbell jangled, announcing another customer. Glad for the diversion, Claire and I turned and looked as four boys entered the store.

"Two at a time!" the clerk shouted, and pointed to a hand-lettered sign on the front window. Two of the boys turned and waited outside, pressing their faces against the window and smearing it. Their friends pushed past us on the way to the soda cooler. One of them nodded: Taylor Hawkes, a tolerable sophomore.

"Hey, Arden."

"Taylor."

He pulled a bottle of Mountain Dew from the cooler and twisted the cap.

"Are you going to pay for that?" asked Hannah.

"Should I?"

She hid again.

Taylor lifted some chips off a rack. "Party at Rachel's," he said to me. "Six o'clock, her parents are going to Duluth to a concert." He bent down to face Hannah. "You can come too."

"I was supposed to have a party," Hannah said after he left. Claire went limp. "It was my birthday and I was going to have a party. Scott was going to come. But then he got drowned and Mom said I couldn't have the party."

Claire opened a cooler and quickly grabbed some milk. Two percent, a whole gallon, staples for two.

I crouched down to Hannah's size and met her face-to-face. "Do you like manicotti?"

22

"Why can't they find his body?" I was feeding the woman; she could give me answers. "If they can recover bodies from an ocean, why not a river?"

With her fork, Claire made tracks in the red sauce on her plate. "This was good."

"My neighbor was an official Betty Crocker Homemaker of Tomorrow when she was in high school. I'd never heard of such a thing, but her daughters insist it's for real. She's also an electrical engineer and teaches at the technical college."

Claire smiled. "I wonder if all engineers are naturally good cooks."

"Good at following recipes, I bet. Why can't they find him, Claire?"

Her wide blue eyes bored down. They were milky blue and rimmed in long lashes, probably the very thing that enchanted my brother. She sighed and her chest heaved.

Okay, maybe it wasn't the eyes.

They sure didn't charm me. All I could see in them was yet another adult measuring my competence and wondering, What can Arden handle?

She wiped a bit of sauce with her finger, then licked. "They may never find him. If he hasn't been recovered by the spring melt, the chances are good he won't be."

"Why?"

Hannah's soft voice floated in from the living room;

she was singing along with the theme to *Doug*. Good, she'd be hooked for at least thirty minutes.

"The current will get too strong and the water will be too high. Either the body will be carried all the way to Lake Superior or it will be snagged someplace. If it's snagged in an underwater rock hole or crevice, it could be stuck until it decomposes. Or, if it's in a surface snag, well, either way it's vulnerable to scavengers."

Like fish.

"What exactly do you suppose happened that night, Claire? Have you thought about it?"

This time her eyes didn't measure; instead, they practically spat out judgment: Dumb question. "Of course I've thought about it. Thought about how I spent hours that night trying to pretend it was no big deal that this guy I was involved with hadn't shown up for dinner. I've thought about what would have happened if I'd sucked down my pride and called the tavern or called here earlier. I've thought about the last time I saw him and how we argued about his stupid new sled. Have I thought about it? *Obsessed* might be a better word."

"Me too. Mostly I think about the phone machine and how things might be different if he or I had turned it on that day. Usually we do. I know you called. I didn't answer because I was in the tub." Soaking safely in hot water while my brother thrashed and died in cold. "And I wonder sometimes how long he held on before slipping in. That's almost the worst—thinking of him trying to get out, and struggling, then . . ."

We both digested that horror in silence. Claire kept

playing with her fork and the smear of marinara sauce on her plate.

"The area of the river where he drowned is one of the most dangerous spots," she said. "It comes through the bridge with extra force because it's been narrowed, then it rushes toward that lowhead dam. The riverbed is rocky, with plenty of snags and holes for entrapment. More than likely his body was forced by the current under the ice into one. That's where it will stay until the water warms. Do you want me to go on?"

"Yes."

She sighed. "Even just a few yards down from where they found the sled, it's too dangerous for diving."

"When it's warmer?"

"Especially then. The current will be too strong from all the rain and melt. It's hard to believe he tried crossing where he did. There's always that open patch, and the surrounding ice seldom thickens. Scott didn't know how treacherous it was, he wasn't that experienced. I imagine he just thought it was the quickest way to get to my place. Or maybe he was trying to prove something."

"I've had nightmares," I confessed softly.

"About Scott in the river?"

"Yes. I see him slipping into the ice, then rolling in the water. Fish . . ."

"Close enough to the truth, come spring. For now—well, cold water preserves things. I have friends who dive wrecks in Lake Superior. A couple of times they've gone so deep they're way below where any fish live and the water is dead still. They've seen bodies a hundred years old, still dressed. They said they looked like mannequins in a wax museum."

We were silent again. "This is awful," she said a moment later.

"Hard not to think about."

She tapped her water glass with her right index finger. "Arden, did he ever talk about me?"

Careful now. The wrong thing would crush the lady's spirit more than any nightmarish image. I sure didn't dare pass along that he'd said "I don't love her." What she felt was obvious. "We lived so closely," I said, trying to figure out how to say more without hurting more, "that we were careful not to step on each other. Once I got older he really backed off and we didn't share much. No more sitting on my bed to say good-night, that sort of thing." Well, that worked. I could see I'd taken her mind off her relationship with Scott and got her thinking about mine.

"This is way out of line, but . . . how did he teach you about the more personal things?"

"Like girl stuff and sex? He didn't; I'm totally ignorant."

She relaxed, glad I'd joked. For a moment we were both relieved of the awful images. I rose and stacked dishes. "That's where Mrs. D. stepped in."

"Mrs. D.?"

"Jane Drummond, the Betty Crocker. My official guardian. She lives across the street. Her youngest kids are my best friends."

Claire nodded. She swung her legs around and rested them on an empty chair. "The jugglers. Scott told me about them. I suppose I might know more about your life than you do of mine."

"That's a fat fact, all right. Until a few weeks ago I had no idea that my brother was even dating someone, let alone that she had a kid. It blew me away, when I first called and heard Hannah's voice."

She lifted her water glass and sipped. "Blew Scott away, too. I didn't hear from him for quite a while after my motherhood was revealed."

"I guess he adjusted."

"Seemed to. And then . . ." Her head sank into her hand.

Two females on the verge of emotional dissolution. We'd both lost the same person, but no way I wanted to cry with her. We'd just met, after all.

Hurrah for television commercials.

"This is the best *Doug* ever."

Claire and I turned with relief to the doorway. Hannah stood there, beaming, untouched by any nightmarish talk.

Claire held out her arms, but her daughter shook her head. "Why don't you come watch?"

We shifted our bodies to the living room and shifted the conversation to mundane topics—Barbie dolls, new movies, kindergarten memories, whether we wanted popcorn. Even as I chatted, a million questions shot through my head. Who was Hannah's father? How long had they lived around here? How did Claire meet Scott? Did she do her own hair color?

Doug ended and Hannah sprang up. Time to go? No.

"Could I see where you work? Scott told me you make wood things. He said he'd give me one."

"Then I'll give you one, but they're not toys, Hannah. I make mirrors and picture frames, things like that." I brushed her hair away from her ear, and she jumped back and scowled. Dumb move—little kids don't let people touch. "Sorry. Just checking for pierced ears. I make earring stands, too."

"No piercing," said Claire. "Not until she's thirteen."

"Tough mom, huh?" I asked the girl. She nodded and smiled again. "And I suppose she won't let you date, either."

"Yuck," said Hannah.

The shop didn't impress her. I hadn't worked since the night of Scott's accident, so everything was dusty. She looked pretty skeptical until I showed her the latest mirror design. She held the single finished one in her hands. "I love this," she said. Claire peeked over her shoulder and laughed.

The eight-by-ten mirror was made of wide birch molding decorated with six of the red wax lips. "Think it will sell?" I asked.

They both nodded. "A million," said Hannah.

"I don't have a million. Just one. You can have it."

"You should make a million, you really should. I'd buy one. My friend Lindsey's birthday is coming up; I'll buy one to give her. Would you make me one to give?"

Simple request, but I couldn't say yes. I looked around at the boxes of fake gems, the racks of molding, the jars of nails, and the pile of wax lips, and they all struck me as dusty artifacts of some past life. "I'm not sure, Hannah. I guess I'm taking a vacation. Sorry."

Claire carefully pressed a thumb against the blade

of a saber saw. "You've really invested in equipment."

"Not much. It was all here. My father's."

"What did he like to make?"

"I don't know. I don't remember."

"Did Scott just let you experiment with these machines? Pretty dangerous."

"Of course not. Before he let me loose with the power tools I had to take some woodworking classes with Community Ed. He made sure I was safe."

"I love these lips," said Hannah. She raised the mirror to her face and carefully kissed one of the red mouths. She clasped the gift to her chest. Her eyes slid around, checking her mother, then landing on me. "He was going to give me something else, too."

"Hannah!"

"He was supposed to bring me a baseball card autographed by Frank Thomas. That night he disappeared he was bringing it."

Before her mother could gasp another reproof I held out my hand. "He didn't take it! It's still here. C'mon." She and I raced up the stairs.

The cards were still on his dresser, of course. The album lay as before, opened at the center with a few loose cards scattered about, everything slightly dustier than when I'd noticed them a week ago. "This is it, I bet. He must have forgotten it."

Hannah took the card and traced the signature with a stubby index finger.

"Do you like baseball?" I asked.

"Yes, but what I really love is collecting cards. This

is a rookie card. He promised to give it to me. He really did."

"It's yours."

"That might be worth some money, Arden." Claire spoke from the hallway.

"Doesn't matter, especially if he promised."

"He did." Hannah held it by the edges. "He said he was bringing it, he told me so that morning when he called."

"He called?" Claire said sharply.

"Oh, yeah. You were in the shower. We talked a long time. He promised to bring me this and he promised to take me to the Mall of America." Hannah turned her back on her mother. "She won't go there," she said directly to me.

"The megamall is cool. Maybe I'll take you someday."

"Like Scott."

"Yeah, like Scott."

She had her trophies and was ready to go home. Claire made noises about the mess in the kitchen, but I waved her off. "I can clean up. I'm responsible."

Hannah bolted out the front door, unzipped jacket flapping against the cold air.

"Arden, I'd like to talk more sometime, without . . ." She tipped her head toward her daughter.

"Sure."

"Maybe someday after school you could come out to the park. I don't pick her up at day care until five. In the late afternoon there aren't usually many skiers or campers around the lodge and we could talk."

"Fine."

"Al visits. He's out along the river nearly every afternoon and he drops by to warm up."

"Why is he out there?"

"Searching. The ice changes daily. Holes open and close as the wind shifts. He wants . . . we all want . . ."

"To find it before an animal does."

We locked eyes, both held still by the horror of a simple, single word.

It.

23

People were especially nice to me my first day back at school. Lots of kids didn't know what to say, but most of them tried, which meant usually they'd sort of hunch their shoulders and maybe flutter their lips, as if they were saying something, but super-softly. And then some people, usually guys, said way too much, going on and on about how they once saw Scott at the c-store and he smiled and was joking with the clerk, or how Scott had done the brake job on an uncle's car, or they remembered when he came for parents' career day in fifth grade and showed everyone his mechanic's tools. Cody stopped me to say Wow, Arden, too bad, and Man, what an awful way to die.

Yes, I agreed.

By Tuesday morning my life was no longer topic number one, not when it was Winter Carnival week in

Penokee. Pep rallies, coronations, daily concerts in the cafeteria. How much gaiety can a grieving girl take? By Thursday I'd had enough, and I cut assembly. I just didn't care which preschoolers hauled in from the Head Start were crowned junior king and queen. I slipped Jean a note telling her I wasn't feeling well and that they should take the bus home or wait for their dad; then I ditched.

Lousy timing, though. Mr. Mills, the principal, spotted me in the hall just as the band started playing in the gym. "Arden?" he questioned. Funny how a principal can load so much into a single word.

I thought fast. Dentist? Doctor? Oh, yeah: "Seeing my lawyer," I said. "Some things to sign."

That satisfied him. "Of course, of course," he said softly. "There must be so many things to do. Do you have a note?"

"Who's supposed to write it?"

He looked around, as if to check for witnesses, then cupped my elbow and led me to a bench outside the office. We sat. "Mrs. Rutledge told me about the agreement to allow a trial emancipation," he said.

"I'll be living alone."

"She is, of course, the high-school liaison to the county's child-protection committee and is in the best position to judge these things. She recommended to me that the school cooperate with your emancipation."

I knew what he wanted to hear. "I appreciate the support and the trust."

"Yes, trust." He rose, claiming a power position. "Don't abuse it."

I didn't put it past him to check with my lawyer, so I

drove downtown. When I walked into John's office, the secretary slammed down the phone and shot to attention. She wasn't that much older than me, and I thought I remembered her dating one of the Drummond boys, but I couldn't remember her name. I announced myself, and she fluttered nervously.

"He's at the courthouse," she said. "He'll be back soon. You didn't have an appointment, but I know he wants to see you. Could you come back at one-thirty?"

"Would you cover for me if Mr. Mills calls from school?"

"Is old Mills on your case? Sure, I'll cover anytime."

Main Street, Penokee, had six empty storefronts, a Ben Franklin, one hardware store, two optometrists, a thrift shop, a dentist, and four cafes. Hard to shop for anything in town, but you can always eat. I picked Lena's Homestyle Grill. Homestyle—they'd have to give me a spoon and let me eat out of Tupperware.

I slid into a booth in the rear, and sat with my back to the door. BREAKFAST ALL DAY, a wall sign boasted. A shadow hovered. I looked up at Lena herself. "What's good today?" I asked.

She didn't have to think. "Huevos rancheros. Always our best."

"Perfect," I said. "And coffee."

"You don't want coffee, honey," she said firmly. "You need juice." And that's what she delivered with the eggs.

I was wiping up the plate with the last bit of tortilla when John appeared. He dropped his briefcase on the banquette and unwound a scarf from his neck. He hung his coat on a rack and sat down. "Care to join me?" I said. Lena appeared with coffee for him. "I'd love some of that," I said. She hustled away, shaking her head. "No tip for her," I said to John.

He nodded. "Some time ago she decided I should drink decaf and now that's all she'll serve me."

"How did you find me, or is this an accidental meeting?"

"Britt told me you stopped in and had gone out for lunch."

Britt, yes. Tyler Drummond's senior-prom date.

"This was the second cafe I checked. Can't go too far in Penokee."

We both meditated on the truth of that for a moment; then he opened his briefcase. "Do you mind talking here? We could go back to the office, but I'm starved. By the way, Harold Mills called from the school to check on you."

"I guess I need to write notes for myself in the future."

John wasn't in a joking mood, not with a briefcase at hand. Like Al, he had been a high-school friend of Scott's, one of the few my brother made during his single year at Penokee Senior High. They'd renewed the friendship when John returned to Penokee after law school.

"Have you had any trouble getting cash this week?"

"Haven't needed any."

"Well, things are clear with the bank. You shouldn't have any trouble now. I've gone ahead and set up automatic payments for your household bills. Here's a list.

Just sign by the X above your name. I could even arrange a monthly account for groceries."

"I can budget for my food, John."

"Fine. I've gone over the bank records for the past year to get an idea of a necessary budget. The two of you weren't lavish, but you lived comfortably. It looks like your household expenses and more were covered by the income from the trusts established for each of you under the terms of your parents' estate. Scott's salary flowed right into the joint account, but it was just gravy; you two didn't need it for anything but fattening up mutual funds and restoring the 'Cuda."

"And buying multiple snowmobiles." I eyed his coffee. Did I dare sneak a sip? I glanced toward the counter, where Lena watched. I drained my juice.

John kept talking money, explaining how he would monitor my check writing and charges. I frowned. "You'll be watching my spending that carefully?"

He nodded. "That's my job."

I tipped my head against the seat back and stared at the mounted deer head hanging over the back wall. Okay, I was an orphan and he was a lawyer with a license to snoop. But did he have to review everything? What if I bought a few things at Victoria's Secret? It wouldn't be long before this guy would know where I'd been, what I'd done, what I was wearing under a turtleneck.

From now on I pay with cash.

"Arden, please take a look at these figures. That bottom number is what Mrs. Drummond and I estimate you'll need for a monthly stipend."

"If I need more?"

"Then we consult. It's our responsibility to see that you have what you need for college. Oh, and I've ordered new checks for you on the household account."

Without Scott's name.

He handed me a few more papers and watched as I signed; then he rose, satisfied with our meeting. "We're finished."

My future, finished.

He rose and wrapped himself against the cold, patted me on the shoulder, and left. I folded my hands and stared at the table.

Lena appeared, her heavy perfume less stealthy than her rubber-soled step. "Here, sweetie," she said, and she slid a cup of dark coffee before me. "You look like you need this."

This is what it's like to be alone in a life newly shaped by death.

You hear sounds. The refrigerator kicks in and hums softly, but it's loud enough to rouse you out of the trance. You discover you're sitting in the kitchen and it's two A.M.

You don't eat much. Milk goes bad.

Homework talks back. There's the open history book. *Don't bother*, it says. There's the sheaf of math assignments. *Screw this*, it says.

You leave lights on at night. Still, you see things in the shadows.

Television becomes your friend. You soon have a favorite infomercial and a favorite Stooge. You watch lots of MTV, of course, because it's on all night. You start wondering about those glistening hairless chests on rock musicians. Do they hot-wax? The next channel over is weather. You watch that, too. Forty below in Cut Bank, Montana, yesterday. More snow in Buffalo today. Rain and flooding in Ada, Oklahoma. Rain—in *February*. You look out the window at your own snowy yard and spend time thinking about the wonder of this.

And once or twice the phone rings, startling you, and you discover you are in his room, on his bed. You are holding his sweater and your face is wet with tears.

25

"You need to get out," Jean said.

"I do get out. I've gone to school every day for a week now."

"I mean *out* out. Do something. Breathe fresh air."

I sniffed. "It is kind of stale in here. I made an omelet last night and used lots of onions."

"Ms. Penny called Mom this morning to say that you're really behind on work. I wasn't supposed to hear, but sometimes it's hard not to."

"Especially when you're listening on an extension."

"I'm not that bad. Mom just has this way of repeating out loud the things she's hearing. She's not sure how to deal with your school problems."

"I'm sure not; she's never had any practice with you and Saint Katherine."

"Arden, I know I'd never want to live alone, but since you do, I'm trying to help. You've got a lot of people involved in this little experiment, and I—"

"Experiment? It's not an experiment, Jean. It's my life. My one-and-only orphanous life."

"Orphanous?"

I shrugged. "It sounds like it should mean something."

She picked up an apple from a bowl of aged fruit on the table and started tossing it from hand to hand. "You can play hermit, Arden, but if you mess up school, they'll clamp down fast."

"I missed nine days of school and people are surprised I'm behind? There's no crisis, Jean. Tell your mom I'll take care of it."

"They may not let you slide on things like Scott did."

"Scott didn't let me slide, he let me be responsible for my own . . . responsibilities. Tell your mom I'll do the damn assignments." I grabbed the apple away from her. Usually the unconscious juggling didn't bother me, but right now I might have tied her hands with a rope if there'd been one near.

"It's not just school that has everyone worried. You don't look good."

Time to confess, with caution. "Don't tell your mom, but I haven't been sleeping."

"Maybe you should take something."

"I don't think the orphan committee would approve of drugs. Or if they did, what do you want to bet your mom doles them out, one each night?"

"She'd trust you, Arden. No one thinks you're that depressed." She picked up an orange and rolled it on her thigh under her palm. "Are you?"

Like me, Jean is committed to wearing no makeup—only it works better for her, with her long lashes and softly flushed cheeks. Everything's round on her face: mouth, cheeks, nose. Right now the eyes were the roundest circles of all, grown huge in loving alarm. I handed back the apple, and without any sign of conscious thought, she started tossing the apple and orange, two streaks of color across her lap.

"Jean, I'm not going to hurt myself out of despair. I'm just tired."

"That's all?"

"Scared, sometimes."

"Maybe you should talk to someone, Arden. Lots of people do. Mom could help you find a therapist."

"There's no way I'm going to invite another adult into my life."

"There must be something you can do."

The recent heavy dose of TV had done more than pass time and fill up the empty house with noise. Thanks to all the babbling and jabbering on the various talk shows, I'd picked up new vocabulary. "Sure," I said. "I can face my demons."

We parked by the bridge, angling the car into a wide spot on the shoulder of County Road JG.

"Do you really want to do this?" Jean asked.

"You can stay here and keep warm."

She sighed and opened the car door. All the heated air was immediately sucked out. Two above, the radio had said just before slipping into a Cibo Matto song.

We slid on our butts down the incline to the river, where we found a narrow path that had been formed by animal tracks and the multiple impressions of snowshoes. Snowshoes were a good idea; too bad I didn't have any or know how to use them. We hadn't even walked five feet before I tumbled through the crust of snow. I grabbed on to a bush and hauled myself up.

"How far do you plan on walking?" Jean asked.

I pointed to a big outcropping of rocks maybe a quarter mile away. "That far."

We made it through the snow and brush with only a few more spills; then we climbed up onto the largest of the rocks. I was panting hard. "Out of shape," I said.

"No kidding. Your face is really red." Jean packed a few snowballs and set them in motion. I leaned back on my arms and looked around. At this spot the river widened to the size of a small lake. No sign of the rapids and rocks that attracted thrill-seeking kayakers in spring and summer. Just a sheet of snow-covered ice dotted by a small patch of open water near the bridge.

"Doesn't look that dangerous," I said.

"You aren't thinking of going out, are you?" She misjudged a toss and a snowball landed at my feet, exploding.

I shook my head. "Just looking."

"Don't look too long. Once we sit still we'll cool down fast. The sun has disappeared."

"The divers must have found his sled somewhere

around there." I pointed to a spot a few yards downriver from the bridge. The snow cover was white but shadowy, as if it were only a thin layer over something darker, something like black water. Why couldn't they find him? How far could he have gone?

Jean was packing another snowball, but it fell apart in her hand. She gave up and hugged her knees. "It's cold, Arden."

"Then let's keep moving. Let's walk along the river."

"I guess it's not that cold."

Someone was approaching from downstream, a bright-red splotch against the white-and-gray background. The figure waddled slightly in a snowshoe step. In a moment the red splotch was followed by a green splotch, also on snowshoes. The couple stopped with their backs to us. The taller figure pointed to something, then slowly turned and let his outstretched arm sweep upriver toward us. The arm dropped when the two were facing the bridge.

Al and Claire. I stood and waved.

They must both have been in good shape because neither was panting at all after sprinting the distance to the rock. I spotted a backpack on Claire, with the distinct outline of a Thermos. "Going on a picnic?"

They looked at each other. "Al was showing me some things," she said.

"Like what?"

Al unbuckled his shoes and upended them in the snow. "Any more room up there?"

Claire did have a full Thermos and—veteran

mother—cookies. It should have been a cheerful picnic, except it was obvious no one could forget the reason we were all drawn to the spot.

"I didn't know you were searching too," I said to Claire.

"My first time out. I had the day off, the weather was right, and Hannah is with friends. Al deserved some company."

"Isn't it sort of futile at this point?" said Jean. "Most of it's frozen solid."

"Not really," Al said. "Mix a little sun with some wind and holes open. It only looks solid." He shifted, crossing his legs. "That's what fooled him," he added softly.

"Did you come all the way from the park?" Jean asked.

"Just from Winker's," said Claire. "We went down as far as the dam; now we're headed back up. It's beautiful on this stretch of the river."

A beautiful grave.

"If you'd been here a bit earlier you could have met Lee Mueller," Al said.

"Who's he?"

"*She* is a search-and-rescue specialist, Arden. She has a wonderful dog that's trained for air-scent searching. The sheriff has called them out twice to search."

"Hasn't there been too much time and snow for tracking?" asked Jean.

Al shook his head. "An air-scent dog doesn't track. It's kind of grisly, though, how it does work."

"How, Al?" I said.

"Bodies give off gasses that rise through snow and water, even ice. The dog can scent those from a distance and follow them to the source."

"Did the dog smell anything today, Al?" I asked.

"No, Arden." He pulled up his long legs and laid his chin on his knees. "We've tried everything," he whispered. "We can't find him."

Claire passed around the Thermos cup again and we took turns sipping. Russian tea, too sweet for my taste; bitter coffee would have been better.

Jean broke the silence. "I'd love to try your snowshoes," she said to Claire in a voice that sounded way too cheerful for the gray day and dark moods. "Would you mind?"

"Not at all. Your boots should work fine in the bindings."

"I'll show you," said Al, and he and Jean slid off the rock to the ground.

"Like this," he said when they had the shoes bound to their feet. He made an exaggerated stepping motion, then started off down the trail, reverting to a normal step after a few feet. Jean bobbled her hands a few times, as if she were tossing something; it seemed to help her find her balance, for she quickly took off in perfect imitation of her guide.

"She's got it. Amazing," marveled Claire.

"She's pretty agile; you should see her handle giant toothbrushes."

Claire shifted on the rock until she was facing me. "This is kind of macabre, isn't it?"

"Picnicking at the graveyard? Yes."

"I hoped you'd come see me this week."

"Busy with schoolwork. How's Hannah?"

"Good. She took the mirror to school for show-and-tell."

"It's one of a kind."

I may not be the world's most perceptive person, I'm probably even a little more self-absorbed than most, but I'm clever enough to sense when someone wants to say something and can't quite get to it. Right now, Claire couldn't get to it. She eyed me, then looked away, then looked back, all the time keeping her hands busy. Oh, she was keeping her mouth shut, but it was all she could do not to burst out.

Help the lady, I thought. "What do you want to tell me?"

"Is it that obvious?"

"Yes."

She picked at her fleecy sleeve. "I haven't told my mother, or my sister, or . . . anyone."

"What is it?" And why the urge to tell me? I wondered.

She had the saddest face I've ever seen, but then she was probably thinking the same about me. Claire extended a gloved hand, but we were too far apart and she let it drop. I had the cup and took another sip of the wretched stuff, something to do, a way to keep busy during her long, discomfiting silence.

She spoke: "I'm pregnant."

God, hot tea sure burns when you snort it up your nostrils, which is exactly what I did. Not a very appropriate response to someone's nightmare news, especially when the liquid ends up all over your face.

Claire laughed and handed me a tissue.

"That's awful," I said.

"Mostly, yes."

"Scott's?"

"Yes."

How long did you know him? I wanted to ask. *How stupid can two people be?* I wanted to shriek. I said, "How far along, Claire?"

"About thirteen weeks."

I counted back. Thanksgiving. I was obsessed with stuffing my first turkey, and big brother was making a baby. "Did he know?"

"Yes. I told him the night after his first accident."

I jerked my head and the movement sloshed tea out of the cup onto my wrist. I emptied the cup into the snow. "Well, that explains it."

"What?"

"His mood. I thought he was depressed and scared by the close call. For days he just sat in the chair and growled. But it was you." Obviously, I didn't make her happier. "Oh, geez, I'm sorry," I said. "What a dumb thing to say."

"He didn't seem angry about it around me. Of course it's not going to thrill a guy—"

Understatement, I thought.

"—but he was pretty positive. He started to talk about living together and marriage."

"Really?"

"Yes, really."

"What an idiot," I said softly. "Oh, no," I said when I saw her look down and bite her lip. "I meant what an idiot to know you were pregnant and then go do this." I waved my arm toward the river.

Claire nodded. "I've been so mad at him. Wall-banging, hair-pulling, pillow-pounding mad at him. I'd kill him . . ." She shook her head.

"If he weren't dead."

"Or if I didn't love him so."

Well, that admission let loose the tears. I handed back the clump of tissue and looked around uncomfortably. Stay or leave? Offer a comforting arm, or the comfort of solitude? Just how close did I want to get?

Claire waved me away. "Al and Jean will be back soon. Go keep them away for a moment, okay?"

"Sure."

"And don't tell, please. I'm not ready yet."

"Of course." I slid down the rock and landed in a mound of snow, falling to my knees. I rose, brushed off, and walked along the trail.

Scott's baby.

I swatted a bush, scattering snow and startling a small bird into flight. It flew out over the river, circled, swooped, and soared out of sight. *How could you?* I howled silently. Wall-banging, hair-pulling, pillow-pounding mad. Exactly.

The trail skirted the riverbank and I jumped off onto the ice. I kicked at it with my heel, sending snow spraying into an arc. Underneath, a sheet of blue-white ice with a hint of black. I kicked again, slamming my heel down on the ice. Kicked at it, and kicked at it, kicking hard at all that was trapped underneath. I moved to another spot and cleared snow with my boot. Was he here? I wanted his frozen, terrified face to appear, locked in the ice under my feet. I'd kick it.

"You stupid!" I shouted.

"Arden!" A voice called. Al or Jean or Claire, I couldn't tell, it was just a voice.

"You stupid!" I screamed. Enraged. Exhausted. Horrified.

I jumped, letting my boots pound down hard.

"Arden, get back, are you crazy?"

A hairline crack appeared under my feet and water seeped through. I knelt and touched it, letting it soak through my glove. So cold. I rose and turned around and saw three frightened faces. Al was on the edge of the snowy bank. He held out an arm. "Come on back, Arden. Move slowly."

Three beers, thin ice, cold water. What a stupid mistake, brother. You were always so smart, but now, just when you're needed, you go for a ride in a blizzard and end up dead, an idiot's death. And now you've left her alone to have a baby. You left me alone. You left—

Words are funny. Pick one over the other, no matter how close in meaning, and it can make a difference. Scratch or claw. Bite or nibble. Shriek or scream.

You died, or . . . you left.

A strong gust of wind blew up snow and rearranged clouds. A shot of sunlight broke through, then quickly disappeared. Just a brief moment of sun, but enough.

Illumination.

PART 2

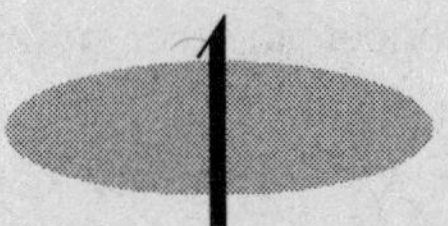

Al put a hand on my arm and coaxed me to solid ground just as the ice under me gave way. Cold water splashed over my right foot. "Are you crazy?" he said. "Does craziness run in the family?"

I smiled at his scowl. "You've got to listen to me, because I've figured it all out."

"You listen to me. We're taking you home."

Jean was there. "You're shaking."

"Of course she's shaking," Al snapped. "She dunked her leg in killer water."

I looked down. Only my boot was wet and dark. "Let's not exaggerate, Al."

Jean nudged me up the trail. I stumbled and fell, and Al turned around and roughly hauled me up.

"Calm down," I said cheerfully. "I'm okay."

"I couldn't believe my eyes," he said as he continued walking. "There you were bouncing around out on the ice. Crazy. Stupid. Just like your brother."

I grabbed the hem of his anorak and halted him. "Was he, Al? Was Scott Munro a stupid person? Before all this happened, would you have ever called him that?"

He sagged. "Of course not, Arden. Smartest guy I knew."

"How many days have you been out here searching, Al?"

"Quite a few."

"Trained search teams and divers, a high-tech helicopter, even a wonder dog. For nothing!"

"What do you mean?"

"All that time and effort, and has anyone found a body? Can't you add two and two?" I looked at Jean and Claire. "Can't anyone?"

"Get her to the car," said Claire. "Now."

"Don't you see? He isn't there!"

They glanced at each other; then Jean put her arm around me and nudged. "C'mon," she said gently.

I batted her arm off my shoulder. "No!"

I was shaking. The wet had leached up and clamped around my leg, while the cold had climbed even farther, dug deeper. "You'll never find him in there," I said, jaw twitching, teeth clacking.

"We may not," said Al. "But we'll keep looking."

"Look all you want, but you won't find him. He isn't in the river. He isn't even dead."

They couldn't get me home fast enough. Warm clothes, hot soup, blankets, and a fire. I loved it. Nice to be pampered. Now if they'd only listen to me.

"I get what you're saying, Arden, and it's ridiculous." Al was still angry.

"Have some soup," I said. "It'll calm you down. Jean, is there enough soup for Al?"

He didn't want soup. "Scott went through the ice,

Arden. Don't cook up some fantasy. We'd all love to believe he's alive, but it isn't so."

"Where's the body?" I said as I sipped. Ummm, wild rice and chicken.

"Arden," Claire said as she unzipped her jacket. She'd been sitting in the background, watching and listening as Al and I talked. "I explained the nature of the river to you." So gentle, so patient, such a good mother. "We may never find his body."

"Exactly. Isn't it perfect?" They all looked at each other. "He picked the perfect spot, didn't he? Scott wasn't stupid to go over that open patch, he was smart. He picked the exact spot where a body would be swallowed up by the river. The *exact* spot where a search would be foiled. Perfect, don't you see?"

"So you say he dumped a brand-new sled and walked away in a snowstorm without anyone seeing?" Al was practically sputtering. "No trace, no tracks. Most important, no reason. Why?"

"The snowstorm covered his tracks and kept other people off the trails." The reason? That was the tricky part. I didn't look at Claire. "His first accident woke him up, made him realize he hated his life here. He was tired of fixing cars."

"She thinks he left," Claire said softly, "because I'm pregnant. She thinks that's the reason."

The bluster went out of Al. He sat down on the futon with me, crushing my feet. I nudged him, but he didn't move. "Claire . . . ," he said as he lifted and dropped his hands. Speechless.

But just for a moment; then he swatted the lump of blankets formed by my knees. "Feel good, kid? You just forced her to pop open a major secret. Does it feel good? And anyway, if you think *that's* a reason, you didn't know your brother. Scott would never leave for that. You obviously have no idea how he felt about her."

"Sure, it's a reason, Al. He was twenty-nine, working a dead-end job, and for the second time in his life someone was dumping a child on him." Okay, I'm an artist with my hands, not with my mouth.

Al rose. "This is ridiculous. I have to get to work."

"And I have to get Hannah," said Claire. I couldn't see her expression, probably because I didn't dare look in that direction.

"I can stay," said Jean. She stepped out of a shadowed corner and took the soup mug from my hand.

"Don't bother. Go home."

"Someone has to stay and take care of you. You've had three weeks of death, hardly any sleep or food, and now it's obvious you're crashing." She leaned down and put her face close to mine. "First you were just delirious, now you're being mean."

"I feel great."

"Get some sleep, Arden," Al said. Claire said nothing. I shifted position and watched out the window as they walked to his car. They didn't talk to each other, though Al put his arm around her. Nothing to say, I suppose.

After Jean left, I was happy to go to bed. For the first time in ages I didn't fear sleep. How could I possibly have nightmares now that I knew the truth?

I absolutely wallowed in deep sleep, not waking until noon. Noon! How decadent. And so's eating in bed, which was what I did as I drew up my list of clues. They were everywhere; how could I have missed them? Okay, maybe they weren't exactly clues. Call them "indicators."

I wrote it all down, scratching and rearranging the events and details. Everything had rushed at me yesterday during that moment on the ice. *Get it straight, Arden. Think it through and get it straight.* I'd show them how it happened. How I *knew*. Then they'd all listen.

City Hall clamored with Monday-back-to-work noises. "Your name?" Police Chief Kent said. "You're telling me you believe he faked his death because of your name?"

"A baseball card?" Deputy Kay leaned on the counter in the waiting room at County Services. "You say you know this because of a baseball card?"

"Ella Fitzgerald?" Peg Raymond hoisted her ass up on the desk at the *Penokee Journal*. "You say you know there's a story because of Ella Fitzgerald?"

"*That's* why you weren't in school today?" asked Kady. "Are you nuts?"

This would be tough.

. . .

"I need your help, John."

My lawyer looked hassled. He motioned me toward a chair and closed the door to his office. "Shouldn't you be in school?"

"I've been working on something. I need your help."

He snorted. "The runaway brother?"

"Yes. How did you know?"

"You're kidding, aren't you? You hit every law enforcement office in town, you go to the paper with this crazy idea, and you don't think I'd hear about it?"

"John, I don't think he's dead. I want to look for him. No one will help. I want you to make something happen. If you make noise, they'll file a missing-persons report."

"No, they won't. He's not missing, Arden. Just dead and out of sight."

"I want to find him."

"We all do, Arden. And with luck we will. With any luck his frozen body will get pushed to the surface in an ice heave, or this spring the water will warm up and the body will decompose and fill with gasses and float to the surface. And then we'll find him."

Tap-tap, tap-tap, tap-tap. Britt typed away in the outer office.

"Arden, even if I thought it was possible for him to pull a stunt like this, I don't see why he'd do it. Sure, Claire's pregnant, we all know that now, thanks to you. But a guy can cope with that without running away."

"Most guys his age haven't been raising a kid for ten years. He must have been tired of it, John." I was tired. I'd spent too much energy and time working on all these people. *Listen to me, believe me*—I'd all but shrieked in their faces. Dead end, again. "He must have been tired of me."

"He wasn't. Hell, you'd be gone in a year! Oh, Arden, don't cry. No, on second thought, go ahead. Let it out. Scott always said you were a tough kid, but there have to be limits. First your parents, now this. You need to go spend a week crying it out."

"I need your help." I yanked a tissue out of the box on his desk and rubbed my face.

He sat back, hands clasped across his pin-striped stomach. "Okay—say he had motive to leave. How did he do it? Running away is logistically difficult. How did he dump the snowmobile without getting wet? How did he walk out of the woods and get away? Where did he go?"

"He could figure it out. It's just the sort of challenge he loves, like putting together a car from scratch."

"That so-called challenge, Arden, breaks a few laws. No way he'd do that; Scott was the straightest guy I ever knew."

"What laws?"

"For starters—endangering law enforcement officers. The county won't be happy about having staged a full-blown search."

"I don't think he'd care. He wanted out."

"Not the guy I knew." John shook his head. "Tough enough to pull off a disappearance, but what about after? How's he going to live? Scott liked nice stuff, Arden. I don't think he'd plot all this just to get away and end up being a bum."

"I was thinking that maybe he stashed some away, in secret accounts."

"Where'd he get it? There are no holes in his trust income and his salary went straight into the household account. I've been over it all. And consider this: Maybe he'd walk out on you and Claire, but leave the 'Cuda?"

"I don't want jokes, John. I want help."

"Here's something we do have to deal with now: Claire's pregnancy complicates the estate. There are legal terms for the situation, but basically, Scott's baby gets his dough. Fortunately, considering the size of your own trust left by your parents, you're still in good shape. Hell, I should retire with as much."

"If he's not dead, you can't go ahead with settling the estate."

"Presumptive death—"

"But I don't presume he's dead and I'm the next of kin."

The phone light flashed, a blinking white eye. I stood up, time to go. Why stay if he wouldn't listen?

John rose. "I'd help, Arden, if I thought it could be true. I'd like it to be so, I'd like him to be alive. But there's no how and there's no why."

How did I know, why did I know my brother was still alive? Simple.

It began—didn't it?—when my parents died. Ten years ago their plane crashes on a tree-covered mountain and big brother comes home and starts being both mom and dad to little sister. Ten years of laundry and stories and cooking and showing up at school, and more than once he cleaned up my vomit.

Just when the end was in sight, a baby. Square one.

Then one day he nearly dies. Cold water is clear water and suddenly everything is clear to him: Enough. Get out.

How could I know he was planning to leave? First, my name. That last morning he'd been so anxious to tell me the story of my name. I hadn't listened, I was too rushed. He begged me to listen. He knew he was leaving and he wanted to tell me that one thing before he left. My name.

I wished I'd listened. If I didn't find him I'd never know. My name. Me.

Then there was the baseball card. Scott would never forget something, especially a promise. If he had really meant to go to Claire's that day, he'd have taken the card. But he left it on the dresser for me to find, sure I'd get it to Hannah.

Ella Fitzgerald. He'd dug out an old CD and played my mother's music, brought all the old CDs out of the basement. "Don't ever forget," he'd commanded. "What little you know about them, don't ever forget."

Because he wouldn't be there to remind me.

Why not just run away, brother? Why not just get in a car and go? Why the sham?

This was the tricky one, of course, but I had an answer: His stunt on the river was the only way that reliable, decent, habitually responsible Scott could make sure that on day two of his flight he didn't bounce back on a bungee cord of guilt.

Suicide, without the death.

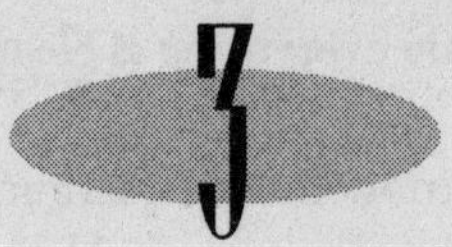

How do you search for a missing person when the police won't help? Some bit of evidence would be nice, something concrete I could drop on their thick heads. But what? *But what?*

"Arden, do you have the answer?"

Damn. It was hard to concentrate on the unification of German states when I was in the middle of a mystery. "I'm sorry, Ms. Penny. Would you repeat the question?"

"I will not. Please see me after class, Arden."

"But I have to go—"

"After class."

I didn't really have to go anywhere, but making excuses to teachers had become a reflex. "Yes, I'm almost done with that paper." "Sure, I'll turn my lab notes in soon." "I really am working on that report." "Of course I can make up the test by Monday."

I stayed at my desk and kept my head down as the other students left the room the instant the bell rang; I wanted to avoid their smirks and stares and sympathetic shrugs. Still, I'd spent my life in school with these people and could recognize them even without looking. Leesa's the one wearing way too much perfume. Bryan has a funny walk, he sort of drags one foot. Tina strides like a diva taking center stage, get out of her way. Jennifer always wears the same noisy, home-made necklace put together from braided leather and clacking tubes of lip balm.

The silence I recognized as well. The weighty nothingness of a teacher preparing to talk. I looked up and smiled.

Ms. Penny was standing so still I couldn't see the motion of her breathing. She was facing the window; then her head slowly turned toward me. Her narrow face was pretty but suffered from a midwinter pallor that was exaggerated by the thin swipes of red on her lips.

"Four inches by evening," I chirped. "That's what they say."

"Yes," she answered. She looked away again, this time toward the door.

Lady, enough games and drama; I have things to do. "What did you want with me, Ms. Penny?"

"Your grade—"

"Pretty bad, right?"

"That's accurate, Arden. I'm deeply concerned."

Oh, weren't they all, weren't they all just so concerned about me? It was like I had this pack of baboons hovering and picking off nits. Pick, pick, pick.

"I've consulted with Mrs. Rutledge and Mr. Mills. We've agreed that I should recommend to you that you withdraw from my class."

"But world civ is a required class. I won't graduate on time without it."

"I'll post an incomplete on your record and you can take it during summer school. Hereafter you should report directly to the library and use this time as a study hall. With effort and luck you can salvage your other grades. You're failing in nearly all your classes, Arden, so consider this a generous offer."

Summer school generous? "Isn't it irregular to give up on someone before they've actually failed?"

"Highly. But under the circumstances . . ."

Ah yes, the circumstances.

"Mrs. Richter told me that your biology grade has slipped from an A to a low C."

"I've missed some assignments."

"As I said, we're concerned."

Pick, pick, pick.

"I realize this has been a horrible winter."

A rocket scientist, this woman.

"During any upheaval, everything seems difficult."

Enough. "Ms. Penny, I should go."

She was bound to have the last word. "During a time of personal upheaval it's important to seek out the things you can control. You *can* control your school performance, Arden. So do it."

Dismissed. I was tempted to salute and click my heels, but I didn't want to jeopardize that incomplete and extra study hall. It really was a generous offer. I grabbed my book bag and gave her a tight-lipped smile. The halls were already empty and I could hear the tinny echoes from the gym where the boys' basketball team was practicing. Jean and Kady would be waiting with cold feet by the car. Time to go.

"One more thing."

I must have slumped, because my bag slipped off my shoulder and hit the floor, spilling everything. Pencils, books, loose papers, erasers, tampons.

"Yes?" I said, ignoring the mess.

"I understand you are pursuing an alternative theory of things."

"I don't think my brother's dead, if that's what you mean. I'm going to find him."

"If there's something I can do to help, please let me know. Distributing flyers, or phoning. Anything."

Posting flyers, I should have thought of that. "Thanks, Ms. Penny, but why? No one else believes I'm right."

"I don't either, actually, but that's no reason not to help. I'm going to Minneapolis on Friday. I'll pass out flyers if you have any. Put them at rest stops and restaurants. That would seem to be the customary way to begin a search, yes?"

Yes. Jean and Kady weren't interested in the idea, of course—especially Kady.

"A wild-goose chase," she said. "I'm not going to pretend I think otherwise."

"I guess I could help," said Jean. "But I need to do some chores first."

"Like laundry," said Kady. "It's your week. And the bathroom is a mess. Your mess."

"Can I move in?" Jean said to me. "Got room?"

I did, of course. Tons of room. But, in a way, there was no space. Everyone, keep your distance.

She was only joking, of course, and didn't wait for an answer. "Want to eat over?"

"No. I've got homework and I want to get started on the posters."

One final night, I promised myself when I got home. One last night for blowing off schoolwork. I had to start the search. Too much time had already passed; people who might have seen him would forget.

I needed a recent photo; head and shoulders would be nice. It was strange, considering I made money on picture frames, but we had only a few photos displayed around the house. In my room I had one of my parents and an old one that Mr. Drummond had taken of Scott and me at a baseball game. Scott had my last year's school photo on his desk and one of him, John, Al, and some other guys down in St. Paul at a 'Cuda rally.

We had only one photo album and everything in it was from before the plane crash. I needed something more recent, and all those pictures were jumbled together in a box. I hauled it down from the shelf over the computer, in the study. As I stepped off the desk chair my shirt got caught on the chair back and I stumbled. The box dropped, the cover fell off, and pictures bounced out. I sat down and picked up a few. Me in a witch costume. Me holding a fishing rod. Me standing on my head. Scott standing behind the damn 'Cuda again. Me, somewhere in the awkward years, displaying a very ugly picture frame. Jean and Kady juggling. Scott eating Cheerios.

I tipped the box upside down and all the pictures scattered. I smoothed them apart with my palm, searching for a face to plaster on the public walls across the upper Midwest.

Bingo. Amid all the color prints, one black-and-white jumped out: a proof for a portrait he'd had taken a few years back for a "Meet Your Mechanic" display in the waiting room at Lorenzo Motors. Same beard, same balding head, same steady gaze I'd seen that very last morning.

Have you seen this man?

He'd hated the picture and wouldn't let me frame it. He'd said it was bad enough that all the customers would see it and no way he'd let me put it up in the house. Said he looked old. Looked mean. He had said he looked dead.

There were only two self-serve copy machines in town and they both cost twenty cents a shot. Even I could do that math. A couple hundred copies at twenty per equaled too much.

The snow was really coming down when I skidded into a space in front of the Ben Franklin. My bumper kissed the car in front of me. Damn. Had John taken care of the insurance? I backed up, parked, then got out and checked. No damage.

The store was deserted except for a clerk who had nothing better to do than watch my every move. She stepped out from behind the register counter and stood with arms crossed as I walked down the office supplies aisle.

My lucky day: copy paper was on sale. Now if my lawyer would only cooperate.

"You want me to do what? Geez and crackers, Arden, I was about to go home. John's gone for the day, it's after five, and I'm the guest of honor at a wedding shower. And I guarantee it, John won't like what you're doing."

"I brought my own paper, Britt. It shouldn't take long. And he doesn't *have* to know."

Britt glanced at the flyer mock-up. I was pretty pleased with it, even though it was nothing more than your run-of-the-mill missing-person poster: eighty square inches of photo and facts.

"You'll be hearing from some weirdos," Britt said. "And they're the only ones you'll hear from until the morgue calls you."

"What a sweet thought and I thank you for it. Will you do this?"

"Sure; the boss is gone."

The snow was still falling, giving an even more desperate and deserted look to the main street. But the lights were bright at the *Penokee Journal*. Saturday was delivery day; with two days to go, they'd be pushing toward deadline.

"I want to buy some ad space for this week's paper. Is it too late?" I stamped snow onto the prickly green doormat.

A woman rose from her desk behind the front counter and smiled. Her glasses dropped off her face and swung on a lime-green cord that hung around her neck. "Never too late for the paying customers. Whatcha got?"

I slid a flyer across the counter. She put her glasses back on and picked it up. She looked at it for a very long time; then she looked at me for a very long time. Finally, she said, "I heard you'd been in talking to the boss. This is your brother, right? You and I have never met, hon, but I sure knew him. Why, Scott was the one I always insisted on talking to every time I took my car to the shop. Trusted him totally. I knew he had a little sister, but I've never seen you around. Funny, isn't it? Such a small town." Her glasses slipped, and she absently pushed them back in place. "I can't do this, hon. Can't help you waste your money."

"That's my decision." I glanced over at her desk and spotted a brass nameplate. Pauline Atwood. "Ms. Atwood, I don't believe it's wasting any money. I should have done it long ago."

She leaned on her elbows and held the flyer in both hands. "Well, it would print just fine. That's a good picture. But, hon, everyone within a hundred miles heard about the accident. Don't you suppose if anyone knew anything different, they'd have called by now?"

I tapped on the counter. I was ready for that one. "Everyone knows the name, of course. The story got lots of coverage, but there were no pictures of Scott. If someone picked him up that day or saw him walking, there was no reason to connect that stranger with the person the sheriff announced was dead. Now they might, if you print this."

She shook her head and clucked softly, still holding the flyer. Then she shrugged and said, "How big?"

I was hungry when I left, and I was pretty sure the only edible stuff at home would need to be defrosted. I circled back to the Woodside Market. Usually at night it's pretty busy, but the storm had kept most people home. As soon as I opened the car door, snow pelted my face and slipped down my neck. He'd left in weather like this: snow piling up about an inch an hour, with a strong wind to mix it up some more. Perfect cover.

I took a bunch of flyers. One I tacked to the bulletin board in the store's foyer, rearranging the hand-printed papers announcing furniture sales and free puppies. I cleared out lots of space around the flyer. No one could miss it. The others I took to the service counter, where a clerk was checking in a stack of videos.

"May I tape these up on the registers? They'd fit right on the back side and it wouldn't interfere with any merchandise."

The clerk took the top flyer and read it slowly, his lips moving. "Hey, this is the dead guy!"

"He's not dead."

"Is too. My uncle spent a day looking for him. It was my cousin's birthday, and he was out looking. That's how I remember. Sure, he's dead. The river."

"May I put them up?"

"Suit yourself."

"I'll need tape."

"Aisle seven."

I bought a deli sub, milk, apples, bread, saltines, peanut butter, juice, cheese, and six rolls of tape. I bagged my groceries and left them in a cart while I taped flyers to the registers. The only other customer was a young mother who was unloading diapers, cans of formula, and boxed macaroni and cheese onto the checkout belt. Her baby, bald and smiley, banged fists against the cart handle.

"I thought he was dead," the mother said when she read the flyer. The baby sucked on a fist.

"He's not dead," I said.

"Did you know that?" the woman said to the cashier. "That guy they were looking for in the river, the one who crashed—he's not dead, after all."

"So what happened?" the cashier said, tapping away at her register while the groceries flowed forward.

"He ran off," I said.

The young mother stared at me, then looked at her baby. She didn't seem so friendly now. "Then he should be dead."

The machine alerted me to three messages when I got home. Mrs. Drummond had called around six because she'd noticed the house was still dark, and an apologetic Walt Lorenzo had called to let me know that someone would be coming by the next day for Scott's truck.

Then Claire. *Please come and see me. We need to talk.*

Did we?

I ate the sub and drank some juice. Not a bad supper, the orphan committee couldn't complain too loudly. They could have complained about the mess, though. I hadn't cleaned for days and had made it all worse by scattering pictures around the living room. I picked up several and tossed them into the box. One caught my eye and I pulled it back out. Scott and I were standing on a dock, a sailboat behind us. I was little and—get this—skinny. I turned it over, no date, no description.

Where were we? Whose boat? Why was he wearing a captain's hat? Who was responsible for that awful swimsuit I had on?

I got a roll of tape, went to my room, and taped the picture above the bed. If I looked at it long enough, maybe I could force the actual memory to the surface. Otherwise, I'd never know.

Not enough. Even if I found it and dragged it up, one memory wouldn't be enough. I got all the pictures and began taping. First I did it without thinking, then I pulled down the ones I'd put up and started over. This time I began with the photos in the album. The ones with my parents I taped on the wall next to my bed until it was papered with pictures. I always checked the back for places and dates. Some were blank and some were detailed: "Arden's first birthday, Ella's Deli, Madison, Wisconsin." Some inscriptions teased, like the one I found that showed Mom and Dad and Scott with a strange man. "With Harry, 30th birthday," she'd written.

Whose thirtieth birthday? And who was Harry? Scott knew him, he was hugging him hard.

Scenes at the beach. What beach?

My father grinning and pointing to a brick building. What building?

A very young Scott leaning against a picket fence. What house? Where?

It was like that thing about a tree falling in the forest. If no one hears it fall, is there a sound?

If no one remembers, is any of it true?

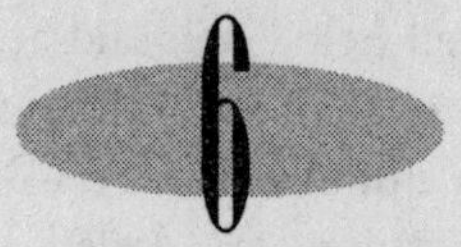

I table-hopped at lunch the next day, handing out flyers to anyone who offered to help. Sure, I knew that most of the posters would decorate the bottoms of lockers and be forgotten, but a few might end up on the wall of a gas station or restaurant. Every little bit, right?

Lunch periods overlapped, and a few seniors were still in the cafeteria. As I moved around the lunchroom, I noticed Jean and Kady sitting together, which was not usually the case. For as long as I could remember, the moment they arrived at school each day they'd split up. At the beginning of the year, if they'd been assigned adjacent lockers, one of them would always swap with a friend. School meant different things to each twin. Kady, who couldn't stop herself from excelling at everything, loved it. Jean was like me: she did well at what she liked and muddled through the rest.

But there they were, together. Or more likely, Kady had joined Jean after eating, because there was no sign of lunch mess where she was sitting.

"What have you been doing?" she said as I pulled out a chair.

"Passing these out." I dropped the remaining flyers on the table. "Want some?"

Jean took the top one. "Pretty good picture. Good for this, at least. Kind of creepy to look at him, though."

Kady wasn't looking. She had her eyes fixed on me. "I think you need help," she said at last.

"Sure do. There are a lot of stores and gas stations in the area. And a zillion bars. If you'd—"

"I meant something else, Arden. I think you should see someone. A counselor."

Jean whistled softly and stuffed empty wrappers into her lunch bag.

"I'm fine. Feeling better than I have in weeks. I'm getting lots of rest."

"You call pursuing some fantasy 'fine'? He's dead, Arden, dead. They found his sled, they found the rope, they found his wallet, and soon enough they'll find him."

"Then I'll be wrong, won't I?"

"You're in some kind of denial. You're wasting your time and money."

"We'll see. Do you want to help?"

She rose and turned to her sister. "You tell her." Then she left.

"Tell me what?"

"Our grandma's in the hospital. She fell last night and cracked a hip. We're all going to Green Bay today after school. Mom wants you to come too, because she doesn't want you to be alone. She told us to tell you so it wouldn't seem like a command."

"Is it a command?"

Jean wadded her bag up into a wrinkled ball. "Mom said yes, Dad said no. He wants you to come, but he's not ready to make it an issue."

"I'll be fine. I've got plenty to do, what with studying and this stuff." I tapped the stack of flyers.

"I think that's why she wants you to come, to get away from things."

"Things like my 'fantasy'?"

She shrugged.

"Do *you* think that's what it is, Jean?"

She tossed the bag from hand to hand as she looked at me. "Life got a lot easier for me when I just gave in and admitted that Kady's always right."

I angrily grabbed at the bag, but only tipped it away with my thumb. Jean's hand immediately pulled it in and resumed tossing. Didn't miss a beat.

"Tell your mom I'm staying home. I can handle a few nights without a watchdog. And I hope your grandma's okay."

Ms. Penny was packing up to go when I stopped in her classroom.

"You'll be glad to know I finished two more assignments during study hall," I said.

"I *am* glad to know that."

"Yesterday you said you'd help."

"Yes."

"I have these." I held out a dozen flyers.

"Of course. I'm on no fixed schedule this weekend, so I've got time to stop along the way."

I fished in my book bag. "Here's some tape."

She took it from me absently as she studied the flyer. "The phone number could give you trouble. You might get some crank calls."

"I didn't dare put the sheriff's number. They don't want anything to do with the idea. I've got a machine, so I can screen calls."

She opened a desk drawer and pulled out a fresh manila folder. She slipped the flyers inside. "He asked me out once."

I nearly peed in my pants. "What?"

"Your shock isn't flattering, Arden. I'm not that ancient, probably only a few years older than Scott was."

Scott *is*. I didn't correct her.

"How old was he?"

Is he. "Twenty-nine."

"Seven years, then. We met three years ago at the library book club."

"I never knew he was in a book club. I wonder where I was."

"Swimming lessons, if I remember correctly. Scott sat in on a few meetings. We were doing Jane Austen that winter. He came for a while each week, but he always had to leave early to get you."

Story of his life.

"One night he called me up, I said no, end of story. I was just bouncing off my divorce and wasn't ready to date."

"I never knew."

She slipped the manila folder into her briefcase. "Well, why would he tell you?"

Scott had tried to date Ms. Penny. What else hadn't he told me? What hadn't I shared with him?

First kiss, first period, monthly bad cramps, crush on my student teacher in sixth grade, the twenty-dollar loan to a kid at camp I never got back, the snotty unsigned notes I used to leave in Jennifer's backpack in seventh grade, the beers I drank at Leesa's unsupervised seventeenth-birthday party. Hey, we all have secrets.

"Get this," I said to Kady and Jean when I met them at my car. "You'll never believe who my brother once hit on."

Jean swatted her hands together and breathed on them. "You really should give us a key, then we can wait in the car."

"Ms. Penny. Isn't that weird? She just told me. Geez, he must have a thing for older women. I wonder who else he dated, or tried to date. I should ask around."

"Leave the dead alone," said Kady.

I was shoveling snow when the Drummonds left for Green Bay. I raised my hand to wave, lifting the shovel, and snow fell on my head. They laughed, apparently thinking I'd done it on purpose. As soon as their car disappeared, I tossed the shovel aside and went in. With their house vacated, my own seemed empty. I closed the blinds and turned on lots of lights. Knowing that the Drummonds weren't watching made it easy to think someone else might be.

Ms. Penny's confession had piqued my interest in my brother's secrets. What else was there?

Scott's room was stuffy, but the outside temp was about ten above so I didn't open windows. I eyed the bed. Had he ever brought someone here, maybe on a night when I was sleeping at a friend's? How much did I really want to know?

His desk had been our parents', one of the few things he'd kept for himself. I opened the top center drawer. Was this where he kept his secrets?

Stamps, pencils, a few more photos of the 'Cuda. The guy was obsessed, all right. I pictured the car in the garage, under the tarp, and thought about how he'd worked on it night after night in the summers, the garage door wide open, light spilling onto the driveway, radio blaring.

"But would he leave the car?" John had said.

The other drawers were just as dull. Receipts, memos from work, sketches of cars. I'd forgotten he liked to draw. He'd taken some classes long ago. Why had he stopped?

The dresser drawers were breathtaking: everything organized by function and color. I hesitated when I opened his underwear drawer, then pushed around the stacks of briefs and boxers. Surely this is where a man would hide something from his sister. The drawers were full of neatly folded clean clothes. He'd done his laundry that weekend. If you were planning to go, why? To throw me off track, of course. Everything had to look normal.

The nightstand had one drawer. Cough drops, a watch with a broken band, two books, John Grisham and Jane Austen. What a combination. No letters, no journals, no pornography, no condoms, no secrets. Absolutely zero evidence of a private life. Nothing. I ask you, how many people could die suddenly and not leave even one embarrassing thing behind?

Had he swept it all away, knowing he was leaving, or had his life really been so bare?

Everything in his room was so neat and tidy. Was it all that simple for him—just get things in order and go? Had he ever hesitated, changed his mind, changed it back?

And now—what was he thinking, doing, feeling? Did he wonder about me, wonder what I was thinking, doing, feeling?

I turned slowly around, scowling at the neatness. All was in order. The only mess he'd left behind: my life.

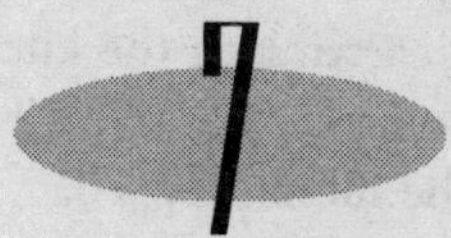

Okay, so life was not exactly idyllic. Still, there was one huge advantage to my situation.

Music. I could play what I wanted, when I wanted, as loudly as I wanted, all over the house. No more headphones in the bedroom because big brother can't be disturbed during *X-Files*. For ten years my parents' first-class sound system in the living room had gone underutilized simply because Scott and I were considerate of each other.

There was another advantage, come to think of it: indecent exposure. From the moment years before when I realized I had breasts, I had never left my bedroom without at least a bathrobe on. Scott, too. Did either one of us ever sit in the kitchen wearing just a T-shirt and underwear? Never. I couldn't even recall him working in the garage on a summer night without a shirt.

Wherever he was just then, I bet he was half naked and blasting music. Like me.

I had the Cranberries cranked up on the CD player, and no clothing on but an old Bob Dylan T-shirt and navy paisley boxers. Both were Scott's. He'd robbed my memories, but I'd raided his drawers.

The loud music was the reason I didn't hear the ringing right away. Then when I did hear it, I thought maybe it was background music, some odd little riff I'd never noticed before. When I saw the knob on the front door jerking back and forth I nearly dropped the mug of tea I was carrying to the kitchen to reheat in the microwave. Someone was trying to get in. I hit the Off button and the music stopped.

I heard laughing, heard my name. "Hey, Arden, open the door!"

Cody Rock.

"Just a minute," I called. I ran to my room and slipped on jeans, slipped off the T-shirt, and put on a bra and sweater.

"Jeee-zoos, it's freezing," a girl whined when I opened the door.

There were five of them on the steps. Cody marched right in. "Sounds like a party," he said. "Who's here?"

"No one." I nodded at the people following him into the house. "No party." I peered out into the night. The Drummonds' house was dark and the Knightleys', the only other house in sight, had a single light on over the garage. Dead-end street, all right. "What do you want, Cody?" I said.

"Place to keep warm. How about breaking out the

glasses?" He lifted a brown bag. The neck of a bottle stuck out.

"That's not a good idea."

"What good's living alone if you aren't going to party? You know Derek, right? And Tianna? A stupid little freshman, but she's okay. This buttface with the six-packs is Rah-nold. Lives in Minong when he's not here in Penokee making his stepmother miserable."

The boy holding the beer made a face and said, "No one's called me Ronald since third grade. It's R.J."

"The *J*'s for joint, right?" said Tianna. "You still got those two we rolled this afternoon?"

"And this is my cousin," said Cody, putting his arm around the other girl. "Abby."

"Stepcousin," she said; then she stood on tiptoes, pressed her face against Cody's, and they tongue-wrestled for a few seconds.

"You've all got to go," I said.

"Why?" asked Cody after he disentangled his tongue. "C'mon, let us stay, it'll cheer you up."

"Let's get the music back on, only none of that chick crap. What else you got?" said Derek. He dropped his coat on a chair and walked over to the CD player.

Tianna went to the phone and punched some numbers.

"What are you doing?" I asked.

"Calling a few people to tell them where we are."

"Don't. You all have to go."

"Lighten up, Arden," said Cody. "Who's gonna know? I heard that your watchdogs are gone for the weekend. Tianna, just in case she's got her cop friend patrolling, be sure you remind them to party-park."

R.J. lit one of the joints and passed it around. I walked to the kitchen and leaned over the sink. Derek followed me and stashed the six-packs in the fridge. "You sure don't have much food." He picked up the phone. "Hey, Tianna, whoever this is you're talking to, tell them to stop for pizza. She's got squat in the fridge."

"Can I get some water?" I was nudged from behind and I turned. Cody was holding up a glass and a liquor bottle. "This bourbon needs to be smoothed out." I took a step to the side and watched as Cody mixed water and bourbon in the glass. "If you really don't want us here, Arden, I guess you'd better call the cops."

I could smell the sharp odor of the dope. I heard the tab pop off a beer can, heard the fizzing, heard laughter and cheers, "Chug it, chug it, chug it." Another tab popped, then, "Oops, there goes half the can."

Time to clean the carpet.

The cops weren't one of my options. Cody knew that, because everyone in town knew I was on a sort of probation. If I had to call the cops to bail me out on a Friday night, what better proof that I shouldn't be alone?

Cody held his glass up to my lips. "Go on. One drink won't kill you. No one will ever know."

"I want some of that," the stepcousin whined. He smirked at me, then turned and handed her the bottle. She actually licked the rim slowly before tipping her head back to drink. She immediately sputtered and spat the bourbon out. "That's crap."

"It's all my brother would get me," Cody said. "I only had six bucks. Man, Abby, you got my shirt wet."

"So take it off." He liked that idea. She helped him with the buttons.

I went to the living room and sat on the futon. Within ten minutes there were three new arrivals. I peeked out through the blinds. There was only one car in the driveway. The others would be scattered discreetly around the neighborhood to avoid attracting attention. Party parking, I'd done it myself.

"You got any good music?" a strange boy called to me as he flipped through the CDs. "What is this stuff? Etta James, Joe Ely?"

"My brother's," I said.

"Her brother's dead," Derek said. He was sprawled on a chair.

"Really? How'd it happen?"

"Snowmobile," said Derek.

"He's not dead," I said.

"Oh yeah?" said Cody. He wandered in, Abby trailing behind, his shirt slung over her shoulder. "Then where is he?"

"What does it matter?" said Derek. "Long as he isn't here tonight."

I closed my eyes and imagined the orphan committee reviewing the situation. I could just picture everyone sitting with hands locked, thumbs tapping together, faces soured in displeasure. *You say you let them in? You say you let them drink? You say there was disrobing?*

Bad judgment, Arden. Just say no at the door.

More people arrived, bringing food and liquor. No

one bothered to knock or ring the doorbell. I knew maybe half of them by sight; the others I didn't know at all. For an hour I floated from room to room, present, but not playing.

"Where's the bathroom?" a boy with a wispy goatee asked me. I jerked my head toward the hall. "That one's busy," he said. "You gotta have more than one." His full bladder couldn't wait for directions. "I'll find it." He spun around and took off, trying every door. Closet, study, my room. I tried to beat him down the hall.

"What's this?" he said, his hand on Scott's bedroom door.

"No, dammit, not there!" I shouted. I didn't want anyone in Scott's room.

Too late. Abby and Cody were inside. "Get out!" Cody bellowed.

"Lucky bastard." The boy whistled and closed the door.

I leaned against the wall and considered my options: go to the living room and join the party; call the cops and forever sign away my independence; play the shrew and make a fuss; retreat to my room and ride it out quietly.

Quiet? Me? My problem had begun because I'd shut my mouth. No more of that.

I pounded on the bedroom door. "Get out!" I shouted. I didn't want to bust in again; a naked Cody was not something I was anxious to see.

"Want your own turn, huh?" R.J. sidled up to me, rolling a beer can in his hands. "Oh, Arden," he added softly.

"Yeah?" I banged on the door a few more times.

"This is really cool of you. It's so nice not to have to drive around and get loaded, you know? Arden . . ."

"What?" I kept my eyes on the door as I rubbed my stinging hand.

"I need to get laid. Do you want to, with me?"

I shoved him a bit as I walked away and he bounced off the wall before sliding down to the floor. I heard him retch, then I smelled the vomit.

That was it. I turned around and walked straight into Scott's room just as Cody was pulling up his pants. Abby shrieked and pulled her shirt down as far as it would stretch. I pushed him toward the door.

"Hey," he muttered, "don't go ballistic. I used a condom, there's no mess on the bed. What's your problem?"

I pushed him through the doorway. He stumbled and stepped right in the vomit. I pounded on his back. "Get out and take everyone with you. You've got five minutes to get out or I call the cops. I don't care what happens to me, I want you all out." I walked down the hall to my room. Just as I reached for the knob the door opened and a boy and girl came out. I'd never seen them before in my life. They blinked in the bright lights of the hall.

"You don't want to use this room," the girl said. "It's weird."

Cody gave me a nasty look, then pushed past and went in. My desk lamp was glowing soft yellow. He flicked on the overhead light and looked around. Two walls were covered with family photos; a third had a row of flyers.

"Get out," I said.

He ignored me. Hands on hips, he studied the pictures, then laughed at the flyers. He ripped one down. "She likes to be watched by a dead guy."

"Get out."

"You're even weirder than I thought." Then he lifted his vomit-smeared foot and wiped it on my thigh. "Hey, everyone," he shouted, "we'd better get going. The bitch has got cop eyes."

The bitch didn't call the cops, but she cleaned house for two hours after they all left. In record time they had managed to trash the place. Cigarette burns on the futon, beer on the carpet, bent blinds on the living room window, pizza on the kitchen floor, splotches of urine on the toilet seat, vomit in the hall, a used condom on my brother's bed. I rolled up Scott's bedding and bagged it with the garbage.

Just as the bitch hit the lights, car tires rolled across the packed snow and ice on the driveway. The engine idled as car doors slammed. I heard soft voices; then the doors slammed again. The car drove away.

Goddamn, they were probably saying. The party's over.

Saturday-morning revelation: I had really screwed up. If the orphan committee found out, all was lost. My mistake wasn't the party, though I knew I'd be hearing from a few concerned citizens if word got to the wrong people that Arden Munro had thrown a good one. And it wasn't the overdue frame orders and impatient ArdenArt customers. It wasn't even the missing schoolwork.

My screwup? Garbage. For two weeks I'd forgotten to put the can out for Friday pickup. A truly responsible orphan does not forget this sort of detail.

I'd bagged up all the party mess before going to bed and left it in the kitchen by the garage door, too lazy to carry it out. So I wasn't hit with the truth until the next morning when I shuffled through the garage to dump the bag in the can. Damn, I thought. Missed another pickup. My errors were piled before me. Good thing it was cold and bound to remain cold; nothing smelled. "Oh, Scott," I sang out when I was back in the warm kitchen, "wasn't it your turn to set out the garbage?"

I'd only just sunk my teeth into the quarter inch of cream cheese glazing a perfectly toasted bagel when the doorbell rang. I cinched my bathrobe and walked into the living room. Nine-thirty Saturday morning, who the hell?

The bell rang again. I was tempted to peek through the blinds but suspected I'd be face-to-face with Cody. I curled one hand around the knob and twisted the dead bolt with the other. Why didn't we have a peephole? I yanked the door open.

Jace smiled at me through the smeared glass of the storm door. The smile faded as he took in my attire and pillow hair. "Did I get you out of bed?"

"Just having breakfast."

"Guess I should have called first," he said.

"No one ever does. Come on in."

He stepped in and we fumbled a bit, each trying to close the door. "I drove my mom over to visit my grandma. She lives in those senior apartments out by the mill. They're cleaning her place and told me to get lost."

"Maybe they could come here next."

He ran the jacket zipper up and down a few times. "Your place looks fine." He sniffed. "Maybe a little stuffy."

"I had some guests last night. Long story. Want a bagel?"

He did. I sent him to the kitchen with directions to feed himself. Time for my shower.

It was a quick one. After all, who dared to spend too much time naked and wet when the only other person in the house was a seriously attractive guy? Not this orphan.

"You look different," he said when I joined him in the kitchen.

"Clean and damp."

"It's the hair. I didn't realize how long it was and I guess I've never seen it loose like that. Don't you usually have it braided and sort of wrapped around? Long as I can remember, even back to fifth grade in Mrs. Belton's class, you've worn braids. Kind of unusual."

"You should see me in a pompadour. Want some more juice?"

He shook his head as he tongued some bagel out of the deep pockets of his mouth. I looked away. I couldn't help thinking about the similar work Abby had done on Cody last night.

"Have you seen the newspaper today?"

I snapped my finger. "I forgot."

"My grandma had it." He pulled a folded paper out of his jacket pocket. "Thought you might want to see it."

"I ran an ad."

"I saw. Sure surprised me. I thought, 'Wow, he's not dead.' Then I read—oh, here, you look." Jace handed over the paper. "It's across from the editorial page."

Op-ed page, the big-time papers called it. In the *Journal*, though, it was just another page filled with local stuff, usually short articles about visiting relatives, school events, and senior bus trips. Today there were quite a few ads, mostly for restaurants and beauty parlors.

And a missing brother. "Perfect," I whispered.

"See the article?" Jace said.

I checked the headlines. Doyles to Celebrate 45th; Open House for Pastor Severt; Local Family Leaves for Russian Mission; Deputy Disputes Theory.

"It's a rumor with no foundation," Sheriff's Deputy Felicity Kay told the Journal. *"On February 3 Scott Munro had a terrible accident and drowned in the Gogebic River. This is not a missing-persons case, it's a fatal accident. This department and other law enforcement agencies are treating it that way. The surviving family members are free to pursue their own ideas, but this agency sees no reason to cooperate because there is no evidence to suggest a disappearance and plenty of evidence that tells us otherwise. Scott Munro is dead."*

"He's not dead," I said.

"Do you know something the cops don't?"

I folded the paper, pressing hard on the creases. "She practically called me a wacko."

"She didn't say anything like that, Arden. But tell me why you think he's still alive."

"I don't 'think,' I know."

"Then tell me."

I told him, and as I talked, his expression didn't change a bit, not one twitch, not one flicker. Stone face. He didn't believe me, either.

"Just take off, Jace," I said. "Go help your mother scrub a floor. I've got lots to do."

"I can help you."

"Why bother? It's obvious you think I'm crazy."

"I don't."

"Then what do you think?"

"I think . . . you want your brother back."

"And so you'll humor me until I've worked through my little fantasy. Well, don't patronize me, okay?"

"I'm not."

"Then go."

"Where? To a cramped apartment where I'll end up washing miniblinds? Look, Arden, you've got a project and I have time. Let's do it."

According to the phone book there were eleven c-stores, twenty-four taverns, and nineteen service stations in the area. We focused on the ones along the roads running nearest the river, and on the two main highways leading out of town. The tavern owners were the grumpiest, but only a few refused to put up the flyer. One bartender actually said missing-person posters depressed his customers. Three men already at work holding down his bar stools puffed on their cigarettes and nodded in agreement.

At the c-stores Scott's face usually joined a few others on the front windows. Almost everywhere we went there were identical circulars for a pair of six-year-old twins and one for an older girl, Janelle, an "endangered runaway." I felt lucky. Scott was missing, but not in danger.

At one gas station back in Penokee the clerk refused the poster. "I read about that today in the paper," he said. "Deputy says he isn't missing. I've got enough cluttering up my windows without putting up something that doesn't need to be there. Go on, now."

We ate a late lunch at Lena's. Once again she wouldn't give me coffee. She just looked at our faces—whipped red from walking up and down Main Street, where we'd taped posters to windows on deserted stores—and delivered two mugs of hot chocolate. "How 'bout some enchiladas to go with that?" she said, and walked away before we could answer. Mexican food with hot chocolate. Jace and I exchanged looks and smiled. Made as much sense as anything.

Jace tapped his knife against the water glass. "I've been thinking."

"That can be dangerous. About what?"

"This flyer."

"Jace, you've been a good sport. Don't start hassling me."

"Uh-uh. Now that you've dragged me all around the county I'm starting to get into it. It's the flyer itself I'm thinking is wrong. Here, look at it carefully." He lifted off the top one from the stack and set it in front of me.

"It's my brother. So?"

"It just occurred to me that we're looking for the wrong guy. This might be a waste."

"What do you mean?"

"If Scott really isn't dead, what's the first thing he did after faking the accident?"

"Got in a car and drove away."

"No. Think about it."

"I have, Jace, that's all I've been doing for days."

"The beard, detective girl, the beard. If a guy with this much facial hair runs away and doesn't want to be found, first thing he does is shave."

I closed my eyes. "He had it the morning he left."

"Of course he did, that's how he wanted to be remembered."

The enchiladas arrived, borne on the arms of a beaming Lena. Jace took a quick bite of his and his eyes widened.

"Hot?" I asked.

He sucked in air through his mouth and nodded.

"Pepper-hot or heat-hot?"

"Pep-per," he breathed. He took a long drink and exhaled. "These are great," he said, and took another mouth-stuffing bite. "Scott was at that tavern before he disappeared," he said through a full mouth. "Did anyone mention he'd shaved?"

"Not that I've heard. Are you saying that between the time he dumped the sled and walked to the road he stopped and shaved? It was practically a blizzard."

He shrugged and cleared his mouth with water. "He

wouldn't dare be recognized. I think you should put up pictures of him without a beard. Got any?"

"You mean start all over?"

"If you have to."

"He's had the beard for years. He was kind of vain about it. He grew it when he started losing hair on top."

Jace nodded. "Lot of guys do that. Me, I'll never go bald." He ran his hands over the short dark bristle on his head.

"Now I'm discouraged."

"And after he shaved, how do you figure he got away?"

"I don't know."

"No one but Scott knows. What do you *think*?"

"He must have had a car stashed somewhere. He didn't use his own."

"Where was it stashed? Where did he get it from? Buy it? A rental? Is there a credit card record?"

"I don't know, Jace. I don't know."

"Have you checked on these things, Arden? I mean, maybe he took a credit card and he's using it all over the country. Have you checked? If he used it to rent a getaway car and the charge shows up on a bill, then you have the proof you need to interest the sheriff."

"I don't think he'd be that careless, but I guess I'll check."

"And how did he even get to the road from the river? The snow is pretty deep and just to walk through it would take ages. A guy running away doesn't have that time. Did he have snowshoes? Are they missing? Did he buy some? Where?"

"He's never even tried snowshoeing, as far as I know."

"So how'd he do it, then? And how did he dump the sled into the water and not fall in? Okay, that's easy—just jump off and send it on. So getting the sled into the water is no big challenge. But wasn't there an ice claw stuck in the ice where it wasn't very safe? How did he set that up?"

"Obviously, there's lots I haven't figured out." I bit down into the hottest pepper ever used by a cook in the state of Wisconsin. Tears immediately spilled over onto my cheeks, but they'd been there long before I tasted the enchilada.

"You okay?" he asked after I'd taken a long drink. His voice was so soft, the tone was an apology.

"I feel so stupid. I hadn't thought of any of it. I'd worked out in my mind why, but not the details of how he actually did it. Some help you are. Now I feel like giving up."

He left his side of the booth and moved next to me. An arm dropped on my shoulder, a hand pulled me in, his head hovered over mine. One kiss, another, a third. "You just feel crummy because you're hungry," he whispered. "Eat."

Lena arrived, commented on our new seating arrangement with a raised eyebrow and smile, and without asking, took away our empty mugs and returned with refills, each topped with a tall pile of whipped cream. My frothy tower wavered as she set it down, then spilled over onto my plate. Whipped cream on enchilada. Only in Wisconsin.

"The old pictures I have won't be any good," I said.

"He's hardly recognizable with all the hair he used to have. I agree, though, that it makes sense we should be looking for a clean-shaven guy."

"I can fix it."

"How?"

"Computer. At school we have a great art program in the lab. Give me one of the flyers and an old picture without the beard. I'll scan them both and make a composite. Easy."

"I'll have to make new flyers and put those up everywhere. Buy a new ad."

Jace smiled and shrugged apologetically.

Square one. Meanwhile, Scott was slipping farther and farther away, as surely as if he were rolling in the river current toward the huge, unyielding grave of Lake Superior.

It was threatening more snow when we returned to my house. "Are you heading back to Moose Lake or spending the night with your grandmother?" I asked as we approached the front door. I fished in my pocket for keys.

He blew on his bare hands. "Mom's the church organist; we can never be gone on Sundays. And I've got some history cramming to do, it'll take the whole day tomorrow. Plus, there's play auditions on Monday and I need to come up with a song. They're doing *Camelot* and I'm going for it."

"You can sing?"

"Not that great, but I look good in tights."

I laughed and dropped the keys. Jace picked them up and unlocked the door.

He waited in the foyer while I went to my room for the photo. As I studied the pictures on the wall and debated which to use, I could hear him humming. When I returned, he had his eyes closed and his head tipped back against the wall.

Square jaw, strong neck, broad shoulders . . . He opened his eyes and we looked at each other. An adult-free house, a good-looking guy. Hmm, what happens next?

He lifted the photo from my hand and laid a chaste kiss on my cheek. "Gotta go. Be in touch."

He ran down the steps toward his car, waving both hands. I closed the door and locked myself in.

On Monday I was pink-slipped in algebra. Normally this is not an earthshaking event. Everybody gets summoned to the office a few times a year, usually to pick up money or a band instrument or forgotten homework a parent has delivered.

Arden Munro to office after third period. I read it over a dozen times during the remaining ten minutes of math. I had no one to make emergency deliveries, so I was pretty sure this wasn't about the lunch bag I'd left on the kitchen table.

Mrs. Rutledge held out her hand when I walked into the office, but I was primed and pumped to preempt any lecture. "If this is about my missing work," I said immediately, "you'll be glad to know I spent all day yesterday at it. I've turned in three math worksheets today, I made up a bio test, and I'm caught up in English."

"Arden, that's marvelous! But I don't want to talk about your work. Would you please come into my office?"

I had a choice?

A tall woman with silver hair rose from her seat when we entered. Mrs. Rutledge shut the door and we all sat down. I sneaked another look at the stranger; she caught me and smiled.

Mrs. Rutledge wasn't smiling, so I knew something was really wrong. Normally, she was so chronically cheerful you wanted to shoot the woman. Not now. "Arden, this is Dina Peabody. Dr. Peabody is the district's new staff psychologist."

I let my book bag fall to the floor; it made a good loud thump. I didn't take my eyes off Mrs. Rutledge, not even when the doctor held out her hand to shake. "I hope she didn't have to drive far," I said. "Terrible to waste her time."

Mrs. Rutledge murmured some soft nothings and fluttered her hands, all to show that she was leaving and I'd be alone with the psychologist. She closed the door ever so gently, then undoubtedly rushed away to the office coffeepot.

"I drove from Ashland," Dr. Peabody said. "Not far. I actually work for three districts."

"Then you have quite a few students who need you more than I do."

"I've been briefed on your situation, Arden. I'd offer my condolences, but I gather you don't think them necessary."

"I think I'm abandoned, not bereaved."

"Then I'm sorry about that. It's a loss too."

"Why are you here, Dr. Peabody? Obviously, the school thinks I need help, but it's been that way for weeks. What's happened now to bring you here?"

"Mrs. Rutledge called me at home on Saturday. She was deeply concerned when she saw your ad in the paper and the article accompanying it. She thought it was time I see you and evaluate the situation."

"You mean she wants you to check and see if I'm nuts. Well, go ahead."

"This morning I spoke with the deputy sheriff. I needed to hear her description of the, um, case. I did. Now I want to hear from you why you think your brother is alive."

I rose, hauling the chair up with me, and made a robotlike turn in her direction. Face-to-face. Let her look me in the eye and search for madness. "He was too smart to have a second accident. He left no embarrassing secrets behind. He was almost thirty and must have felt buried alive in a life he hadn't chosen. With a baby on the way, the final nail was about to be driven into the coffin. He had too strong a conscience to just walk out. He'd promised a friend he'd give her something, then he left it where I'd be sure to see. He had this sudden urge to tell me about my parents and tell me about my name."

"That's it?"

"There's no body."

"Your parents' bodies were never returned to this country, isn't that right?"

A good punch. My breath returned in a minute. "This isn't about my parents."

"It might be."

"It's not. And yes, their bodies were never recovered from the crash site because the terrain was too wild. My mother and my father were left to rot in the jungle, if that's what you want me to say. I don't suppose it took too long in that climate and with all those jungle critters."

"Was there a memorial service?"

"No."

"Why not?"

"What exactly do you want, Dr. Peabody?"

"To help you."

I just shook my head slightly.

"No relatives?"

"They were both only children."

"Family friends?"

"Some, I guess. I was pretty young. Scott would have known them, but they've faded away."

She burped softly into her wrist, then pressed fingertips to her breastbone, or the spot where a breastbone was undoubtedly hidden under her large breasts. "Sorry. I had a rather spicy breakfast at a cafe in town."

Lena strikes again.

"Were your parents from this area?"

"East Coast."

"Why did they choose to live here?"

What had Scott told me? "They liked the northwoods. Dad practiced in Rice Lake, Mom in Ashland. This is sort of halfway."

"When did they move here?"

"When I was five."

"And Scott was . . . ?"

"Older."

"He didn't grow up here?"

"Dr. Peabody, I understand that I have to cooperate with you because I am legally a minor and I have all these people mucking about in my life who will screw me over if I don't. But I don't want to talk to you about my childhood, or my brother's childhood, or my parents, or what their corpses look like by now."

"Your parents—"

"Are you having fun, Doctor? Do you enjoy this?"

"Your anger tells me a lot, Arden."

My anger. That's what she wanted, of course. To poke and prod at me until I cracked, blew up, cried, punched, howled. Then they could say, Poor girl, she's not doing well. And the things she's imagining!

I wouldn't give them the chance. I smiled. "What does it say?"

"It's a form of grieving."

"Could you explain?"

She did, of course, delighted to show her stuff. She talked on and on. I smiled and nodded, chewed on my lip, feigned contemplation, laughed a bit when she did.

All in all, a great performance. When she finished, she motioned to me to speak.

"You've given me a lot to think about," I said.

"I'm sure."

"I feel a little wiped out."

"That's to be expected."

I twisted my hands, then folded them tightly. She noticed and leaned toward me expectantly. God, wouldn't she love it if I cried?

"Do you suppose . . ." I let my voice break and took a deep breath. "Do you suppose it would be okay if I went home? I mean . . . I feel . . ." I stopped and let my head drop.

It was all she could do not to lunge and hug. "Oh, of course. I'll clear it with Mrs. Rutledge."

"Thank you." I picked up my bag and gave her a tight-lipped smile as a farewell. I let my shoulders slump as I walked out.

As I said, a great performance.

The first thing I did was pick up lunch at Lena's, a Coke and a burrito, easy on the peppers. Then I gassed up the car and headed out of town.

Scott could have taken a car from the lot at Lorenzo's, but he wasn't that stupid. He had to have gotten one from somewhere else. The best bet to my mind was that he rented one and used it to get away, possibly ditching it later. The nearest rental agencies were in Duluth and Superior. The Twin Ports were almost an hour away, but the sky was blue, the roads were clear, and I was out of school early.

If Jace was right about Scott shaving, he hadn't

done it until after he'd set up the details of the accident and escape. Which meant he had to rent the getaway car when he still had the beard. My flyers weren't worthless after all.

The major car rental companies had booths at the Duluth airport. I went there first and within a few minutes knew there'd be no hot trail.

"Do you remember renting a car to this guy about a month ago?" I asked several rental agents. A month ago! they'd gasp. You kidding? Then there'd be a head shake and the agent would say, I don't remember what I had for lunch, or what color socks I'm wearing, or my wife's birthday.

The guy at the Avis booth was a real clown. "Hey," he said, smirking, "I don't remember who I slept with last night."

Ha, ha.

Most of the other rental agencies listed in the phone book were all in car dealerships. I didn't bother. Scott knew quite a few mechanics and service reps in the area. No way he could walk into a dealership and not be noticed.

The one remaining business had a downtown address. U-Save Auto Rental was in an old brick building on a street that ran parallel to Lake Superior. It was tucked between a church drop-in center and an apartment building that boasted a choice of daily, weekly, or monthly rates. An old man sat on the stoop of the apartment building, humming and tapping a cane against a handrail. I hurried past him and opened the U-Save door.

I expected a dark room to match the exterior, but

the office was clean and nicely decorated. There was no one working, so I tapped the silver bell on the counter. A woman poked her head out of a rear office. "Minute?" she called out. I nodded. While I waited, I browsed. There were two chairs, a table, magazines. No bad office art, nothing at all on the walls. In better days, I might have approached them about a custom job, maybe a large mirror with birch molding decorated with an assortment of toy cars.

"Need a rental?" the woman said, approaching the counter. She leaned on it and smacked her lips. She ran a hand over her head. Her black hair was so short and spiky I expected to see blood drip from her palm.

"No, I'm trying to find someone." Out with the flyer. "Do you remember renting to this guy about a month ago?"

She looked at the circular long and hard. She shrugged. "I'm new. The other girl quit. Can't blame her. It's so boring."

Dead end.

"This your boyfriend?"

"Brother."

"I could check the computer for you. What's his name?" She read it off the flyer and typed it in. "Nothing on Munro."

"I don't think he'd have used his real name."

"Ooh, that makes it fun. I love mysteries, they're the only books I read. I used to read Westerns, if you can believe it, but they're all so alike I got bored. I mean, I could write something as good as some of the dumb ones I was reading. Maybe what I should write is a Western mystery, that would be perfect." She stroked her hair again. "I'm Jill, by the way. Okay, what dates are we talking? I'll bring up all the rentals for around then. Maybe one of the names will sound good, like he mixed your mom's maiden name with his best friend's name or something."

What would he choose? I wondered as I scanned the list. What would I choose, if I could name myself?

Nothing looked right, though I had her run the record on Will Ford and Zeke Dodge. "Car names," I explained. "He's a mechanic."

"Good enough reason," she said, fingers flying over the keyboard. She shook her head as the transaction records scrolled onto the screen. "I don't think so. They've both had accounts with us for years."

"He probably would have used cash, would that be a different list? Do you even take cash?"

"We'll take anything the bank will take, but we do need an ID."

"Then it would have to be under Munro."

"Not necessarily. Did he have time to plan his disappearance?"

"About a month."

"You can buy IDs, you know." The phone rang and she made a face as she picked it up. While she talked and arranged a rental, typing speedily with one hand, she reached under the counter and pulled out a gaudy tabloid newspaper that was folded open to a story about combusting corpses. She swiveled the phone receiver away from her mouth. "Don't tell the boss I read on the job," she whispered. Then she resumed making muttered responses into the phone as she riffled through the paper to the last page. "There!" she mouthed, and tapped the paper with a finger.

Birth Certificates, Diplomas, Green Cards, Driver's Licenses. Call for catalog.

Jill hung up the phone, shaking her head. "What bozo would want a convertible in winter?"

"Mail-order IDs? These must be illegal."

Jill leaned on the counter. "If you're desperate, what does it matter?" She looked around, as if someone might have sneaked into the office and was listening in a corner. "I had this girlfriend," she said in a soft voice, "who needed to get away from an old boyfriend, right? God, he was a number. I mean, she had to get out or she'd get dead. Anyway, she calls one of these places and gets the catalog. 'Your name on any state's driver's license,' it says. 'For collectors,' it says. Yeah, right. Collectors—that's how they cover their asses."

"I don't think he'd have dared to order any catalogs. I might have picked up the mail."

She rolled her eyes. "Any dope with a few bucks can rent a private box at one of those packing-and-mailing stores. Have you checked them?"

"No. Good idea."

"Let's make a list. You can check them out after you leave here. They might not want to tell you anything, but you've gotta try. God, this is fun."

Glad someone thought so. I paged through the tabloid as she leafed through the phone book. I started reading personal ads and her hand slapped down. "Don't you dare!" she said. "Most of these guys are inmates, don't you know that? You're way too young for that. I had this other girlfriend, oh, let me tell you . . ."

I wished I could have taken Jill with me. Maybe her enthusiasm would have helped. There were quite a few rent-a-mailbox stores in the Twin Ports. I hit five and struck out at each; Jill might have charmed someone into talking. On my own, all I heard were variations of the same thing: Get lost, kid.

After the fifth miss, I gave up. Outside the last store, a pay phone half hidden by a pile of dirty snow caught my eye. A tattered phone book hung from a wire. I flipped through the pages looking for Jace's number down in Moose Lake. Might as well take advantage of the in-state rates.

I hummed impatiently through his mother's chirping message on the machine, then left my own message. "This is Arden, I had another idea," I said immediately after the beep.

I only had a few quarters, so I talked fast. Would he take the old flyer around to country car lots in the area? And how about sports stores that sold snowshoes? Were there any places around Moose Lake where someone could rent a mailbox? Hit those, too, wouldja, Jace? Oh, and how did the photo-morphing go? It's starting to snow, thanks and good-bye.

I bought supper in Superior, but it was the worst. The burger was rubbery, the fries were limp, and the soda in the plastic cup tasted like a petroleum product. I ate it all regardless of appearance and taste, and within minutes of consumption it was all roiling in my stomach, threatening to explode. Home, someone please get me home.

It began to look as if I'd never get there. Twenty miles from Penokee it started snowing, nothing too serious, but the oncoming traffic was heavy, so it took ages before I could pass the little old man in the big old car creeping along at forty-five. And after I did, I forgot to slow down out of passing speed. Which is why I now have my first-ever speeding ticket.

"I hope your parents make you pay this fine out of your own pocket," the trooper said. "Be a lesson for you."

"Yes, sir. I'm sure they will," I replied. "They're very strict." And very dead.

The orphan committee would not be pleased, of course. But I could always cite classmates who'd been tagged for worse—shoplifting, possession, underage drinking, driving while intoxicated. What would concern them the most, I imagine, would be that I was driving-while-detecting. Lock her up, Officer.

The Drummonds' house was lit from top to bottom. I debated pulling into their drive instead of my own, but I felt too surly. Besides, they were just back from a trip to her ailing mother, so Mrs. Drummond wouldn't have had time to get to work in the kitchen.

The phone messages logged on the machine only made me surlier. They were all crank calls, or at least useless ones. Two callers asked about a reward. Another guy offered obscenely to take the place of the missing man. A drunk, probably dialing the only number in sight, called from a bar and asked for a ride home. A psychic left the message that she was getting "vibrations" and would be happy to tell me more for a small fee.

I erased them all and then made my own call, to Jace again. "Did you get my message? Did you get the flyer done?" I said as soon as he got on the line.

"Hi to you, too," he said. "And no, I didn't get it done. I don't have art until Wednesday."

"Can't you get in there before then? Time is important, Jace!"

"It's not there for my personal use, Arden; I have to do it as part of class."

"Make sure you do it on Wednesday, okay? And what about my idea of going around to the car lots?"

"That's a lot of driving. I'm not sure I can get the car for that."

"Tell your mom it's for something else, then. Please, Jace?"

"I'll try. How you doing today?"

"Less than great. I was ambushed by a therapist, I got my first speeding ticket, and my stomach feels like it was introduced to *E. coli*. Call me when you get it done, okay?"

He promised, we said good night, I hung up, and only then remembered about his play audition. Never mind, I'd ask next time.

I was in my bathrobe on my way to the shower when the doorbell rang. "How do people know?" I groaned. Another ring, long and shrill. Could I ignore it? I knelt at the window and peeked. No car, probably Jean or Kady.

As soon as I opened the door Mrs. Drummond marched in. Where had I seen that expression before? Ah, yes, the state trooper.

"Welcome home. How's your mother?"

"Stable and comfortable. I'm supposed to be your guardian, Arden."

"That's good about your mom. And I'm supposed to be emancipated."

"Not entirely. I leave for a weekend and within an hour of getting home I hear that you had a party here—"

Yeeps.

"—and that you have spent time and money plastering the town with missing-person posters. Then I hear that today you left school early to come home, but instead disappeared for hours. No one knew where you were. You are pushing the limits, Arden. My limits."

This was new, and I took a moment to savor it. Never in my memory had I received a motherly scolding. Perversely, I found it pleasant.

"The party wasn't much. Some people came by uninvited and I got rid of them as soon as I could." I restrained myself wonderfully and didn't look toward the vomit stain.

She unbuttoned her coat. "That's what Kady guessed. I heard about it when we ran into Paula Rock at the store. She said her son reported you threw—and I quote—a 'good one.' I should never have left you alone, Arden. Next time I won't."

"Next time I'll be ready and won't let anyone in. Things were okay, Mrs. D."

"And where were you today?"

"Duluth. Superior. There were a few things I needed to do."

She pulled a folded flyer out of her coat pocket. "Related to this?"

The motherly scolding was losing its appeal. "Yes."

"Kay Rutledge said you talked with the therapist today. I'm glad. I think it's overdue. I should have insisted long ago."

"Wasn't my idea."

"I don't imagine it was. This is your idea. . . ." She smoothed the wrinkled paper between her hands. ". . . this wild-goose chase."

I'd have argued, but the day's trip had been exactly that.

"If emancipation is going to work, Arden, we need a few more rules. I need them."

That was honest. I smiled to signal possible cooperation. "Such as?"

"I want you over with us more, at least two nights a week. Monday and Thursday would be best."

"Sleep over?"

"That's not necessary, though you're always welcome. Let's say dinner and homework. It will be a time to check in with you and see what you're up to. I want to hear about your activities from you, not from someone I meet at the grocery store." The flyer disappeared into her pocket again. I heard it getting crumpled in her fist. "I thought I could go along with this trial independence, but now I'm not so sure. Years ago I promised Scott we'd take care of you if anything happened."

"You are taking care of me."

She smiled sourly, rubbed her eyes, and yawned. She'd had a bad day too. "Are you getting any calls in response to the poster?"

"A few, nothing helpful." I didn't dare tell her about the string of messages I'd found when I got home.

"If you insist on posting your phone number all over the place, I'm going to insist you get Caller ID."

"That might be a good idea. I should have thought of it."

She cheered considerably. A lesson, I guess: Give them an inch and they think they've won a mile. "We're agreed, then," she said. "You get Caller ID, you join us for dinner two nights each week, and I always want to know when you leave town and why. I think it's a reasonable compromise."

The rubber burger turned over in my stomach. It was a reasonable compromise, especially if it involved home cooking.

Mrs. D. went home pleased. She'd done her part. Now my lawyer could do his.

"You want what?" John didn't sound confused as much as irritated. I could hear the TV in the background, a basketball game.

"All the credit card records, canceled checks, and phone bills."

"Going how far back?"

"The last three months. John, I really can be responsible for my own bills."

He dismissed that with a snort.

"Can I get them tomorrow?"

"Britt will have them ready. *After* school."

Scott and I didn't use plastic very often. Cash and checks, pay as you go. I had a card for ArdenArt, and we had two household credit cards—one Visa and one MasterCard. Three gas cards. Neither of us had much of a long-distance phone habit. Orphans, who would we call?

So the envelope Britt handed me was thin and light. "This it?" I said.

"Copies of all the recent bills. And you don't have to bother calling the credit card companies to see if he's used them lately. John did that this afternoon. There's been no activity in weeks."

So John had checked. Maybe he was coming around, maybe I'd finally convinced someone that Scott wasn't dead.

Britt was a mind reader. "He's cooperating, kiddo, because *A*, the fastest way to stop you is to prove you're wrong, and *B*, the client is boss." She snapped a finger against the envelope. "Good luck, Sherlock."

It didn't take a world-famous detective to see that there was nothing hidden in the canceled checks and the bill records. A simple trail of money, most of it spent on food, utilities, clothing, 'Cuda parts, snowmobiles.

I laid out all the checks. His smooth round script mixed with my angular scrawl. His signature was so familiar; I'd seen it on years of notes to school and notes to me.

Please excuse Arden's absence . . .

She has permission to attend . . .

I thought I asked you to fold the towels. DO IT before I get home.

The phone bills were tougher to decipher because they only listed numbers and cities. Britt had included the bills going way back to September. September was on top and I looked it over even though I knew it would have nothing I needed. I was sure he'd begun planning everything the night of his first accident, the night he found out he was going to be a father. When I unfolded the January-February bill, the long list of black numbers nearly vibrated. At least twenty calls, when it was unusual for us to have three. "Gotcha, you bastard," I whispered.

Right after the first accident there was a flurry of phone activity. Minneapolis, Spooner, Duluth, Ashland. All over. His getaway trail. Fool—he'd planned everything on the phone.

I started checking the numbers, and by the third call, I was back on Earth. He was a fool all right, but for a different reason.

The numbers were all snowmobile dealers. He'd spent sixty-seven dollars on long-distance calling to price snowmobiles.

By the time I'd dialed eleven numbers and eliminated duplicates, I had one left: a three-minute call to Winona, Minnesota. Undoubtedly it would be someplace called the Sled Den or Four Seasons Recreation or Einer's Engines. I punched the numbers.

"Bart's Parts, Bart speaking."

"Sorry to bother you, sir, but I'm just checking on some calls on our phone bill. My brother must have called this number."

Bart thought that was funny and let slip a low chuckle. "Your brother? Not checking on the boyfriend, really, now are you?"

"My brother."

"Well, miss, you'll be glad to know that this is a salvage yard, not a motel or adult entertainment store."

Salvage yard. The damn car. "He has a '70 Barracuda. I guess he was calling about that."

"You betcha. I've had a lot of 'Cuda callers. Ran an ad in the *Trader* a while back for some rocker-panel moldings I was selling."

"That must be it. Sorry."

"You might want to tell your brother that in a week or so I'll have a Shaker hood to sell."

"I'll tell him."

I hung up and double-checked the bill, reading the number and date maybe twenty times. He'd made the call to Bart in Winona on the Saturday before he left. The day before.

For the first time since I'd bounced on the ice, doubt crept in. Just a seed, just a flicker, just a question. If he was about to run, why shop for 'Cuda parts?

For the first night in a long time, my sleep was riddled with bad dreams. It was as if admitting doubt had admitted nightmares.

Fish again. Fish eyes, popping fish mouths, flapping gills. This time I was the one rolling in turbulent water. Scaly, slimy fish bodies rubbed against me, rolled over me. A huge pike approached, spiked mouth open. I lifted an arm to ward it off, then tumbled backward in the current as I reeled in shock: My hand had been pecked and gnawed to the bones.

"Pass the potatoes, please."

My second helping, but then, it was my first good meal in ages. Mr. Drummond beamed as he handed over the bowl of mashed spuds.

"Be sure you take some of that roast home," said Mrs. Drummond. "There's lots."

I reached for the meat platter and caught a glimpse of Kady's scowl. She and Jean had been vegetarian for years, but had long ago reached an accommodation with their parents about family meals. Surely the presence of a tender and perfectly cooked pork loin hadn't provoked her bad mood. "What's wrong?" I asked her.

Jean lifted apples from the fruit bowl and started tossing. "She's menopausal."

Her father rose from his chair with the empty water pitcher and deftly grabbed one apple out of its arc. "Don't use the food."

Kady folded her napkin into a tidy square. "Do you remember the plans we made for summer?"

"I do, but I haven't really given it much thought lately. You can't blame me for that."

"Geep-seez," said Jean, and she started juggling napkin rings.

"This week in the mail I've gotten performance and vendor applications for four festivals. Two in Minnesota, one down in Madison, one in Spooner. Are you still interested?"

"I might be if I thought I'd have anything to sell, but, Kady, I haven't been near my workshop in ages. I have old store orders I haven't even filled. I don't see how I'd have enough stuff."

"You would if you got to work. You'd have plenty of product if you concentrated on that instead of . . . other things."

Mrs. Drummond started clearing the table. Jean rose and lifted the dishes from her hands. "This could get nasty. Go correct tests, Mom."

"You guys can do it without me," I said. Not true; I knew my car was essential.

"Don't want to," said Jean.

"I'm sorry I've screwed up your summer. No—I'm sorry my brother screwed up our summer."

Kady poked at the bean loaf on her plate. "Have you had any luck with the flyers?"

"No."

"What next?"

"I don't know. I've sort of run into a dead end."

"Bad joke," said Jean, and she exited with another armload of dirty dishes.

"Have you thought about getting a detective to help?"

"I thought you regarded it all as a ridiculous fantasy."

"I do. I think he's dead, but if you're going to fixate on it, at least you can do it sensibly."

"I don't need a detective, but there is something that puzzles me. Something that doesn't fit."

"So you've given up?" She looked pleased.

"No, but you could say I've paused."

The message light was blinking when I got home. I checked the number on the ID display. It was a 612 area code, the Twin Cities. Most of the crank callers had been local, and they'd all stopped leaving messages after I taped one that warned that names and numbers were being recorded. This caller didn't care.

Hello. I'm calling about that poster. I don't know if this is related or anything, but I saw something that might help. Probably not; my wife thinks I'm nuts and shouldn't get your hopes up, but my grandfather went missing once, wandered away from his house, and I know the worry. Anyway, I can't say I saw the guy on the poster. But that day in February my wife and I were up at her boss's cabin near Penokee and she wanted to leave some cookies in the freezer, sort of a thank-you. Only we didn't have the right ingredients so we ended up going into town. Actually, I went into town three times that day. The first time was real early to get the paper and coffee. And there was this car parked on the wayside on County Road JG. All day it was there. Drove by it two more times that day. Then when we headed back to the Cities, we saw a guy wearing a red jacket or sweater get into it. Just saw his back, you know, opening the door, leaning in. About four-thirty. It was really snowing by then, so I didn't get too good a look, but it seemed like he would have been about the right height. Dark hair, like in the photo. Sorry I can't help you with the license plate or car model or anything. It was big, did I say that? Dark, maybe blue. American car. A beater. Anyway, I thought I'd call. Probably nothing, but still.

Probably everything.

"Thanks for coming over, John." He didn't look at all happy; I suppose I'd interrupted another basketball game. But the guy was my lawyer, hired help, and paid to jump when the client called. "Just toss your coat in the closet and sit down. I've got cocoa. Want some?"

He nodded sullenly while he leaned over to pull off his boots. "What's this message you want me to hear?"

"On the machine. Go ahead and play it while I'm in the kitchen." I heard the tape run through twice while I was filling the mugs. I spilled plenty as I hurried to get back and see his reaction to the message. I handed him a mug. "Will you admit I was right? Do you think I can get some help now?"

He didn't look elated, didn't look puzzled. Chewed on his lower lip while he stared at the machine. Sipped his cocoa, set down the mug.

"Did you hear it all? They saw a guy. They saw Scott."

"They saw someone."

"Don't be a blockhead about this, John. It was the right day, the right place, they thought the description fit, the guy had a red jacket."

John rose and walked down the hall to Scott's room. After a moment I heard him come back out and close the door. "Like this one?" he said. Scott's favorite jacket hung on a hanger that swung from John's hand.

Red and limp, like a punctured balloon. "It was in his closet. I remembered seeing it when I searched for his checkbook."

"I didn't notice it was there," I whispered.

He laid the jacket across a chair, and the hanger slipped out and fell to the floor. "Do you want some help clearing out his things, Arden? Dead or alive, he obviously doesn't want or need them."

"He was the one getting into that car. I know it."

John groaned and dropped into a chair.

"Of course his coat is still here because he didn't dare pack anything; we would have noticed. But he would need some getaway clothes; he couldn't just hit the road in a leather snowmobile suit. He probably bought another jacket and had it stashed in the car. Makes sense he'd get one just like his old favorite."

Another groan.

"Can't you help me?"

There must have been an especially plaintive tone to my wail; my lawyer sat up straight and crossed his arms. "I'll help by making you face the truth, Arden. Ask yourself some questions. First, where did he get the car?"

"He was in the business, he knew places, it wouldn't have been hard."

"How did he pay for it? There's no record of a purchase and no sign he dipped into his personal accounts for any sizable amount other than for the snowmobile. I've been through everything."

"The guy said it was a beater. Couldn't have cost much. Or maybe . . . maybe he took one off the lot."

"Stole from Lorenzo?" John tapped his fingers and closed his eyes. "Arden," he whispered, "you're not connecting with reality."

"Go home, then. I'm sorry I made you come over."

"I'll do this for you. Give me the number of the guy who left the message and I'll call and try to get a better description. And I'll twist Al's arm to get him to ask around. See if other people at Winker's that day noticed the same car. Maybe they know who it belongs to."

"Belongs to my brother."

He was beyond listening. "Meanwhile, you can do this: Figure out how he paid for this adventure you believe my dead friend is enjoying. It always comes back to money, Arden. How did he finance the great escape and what's he living on now?"

After he left, I sat in Scott's favorite chair and listened to Scott's favorite music and tried to think like Scott. For days after the first accident he'd sat in the living room and plotted. Thinking it through, making up his mind, probably rerunning mental tapes of his life.

His life. When had he started to hate it so much? Had he started to hate me?

John was right about the money. Where had it come from? My brother had figured it out while sitting there. I could too.

From the chair I could see the speakers and CD

player, the bookshelves, the framed museum poster, the futon and coffee table. Several weeks of his magazines and junk mail had piled up on the table, where I dropped them each day. *Cars and Parts*, *Engine Update*, *The New Yorker*, *Sports Illustrated*. An *SI* had slid off the pile. On its cover, bold black letters proclaimed SPRING TRAINING PREVIEW. The picture showed Frank Thomas slugging one into outer space. Hannah would love the photo, it was just like the . . .

Baseball card.

A City of Duluth snowplow was carving out a parking spot on Superior Street. I challenged all the cops in the area and made a U-turn. Just as the plow's driver lifted his blade and moved on, I skidded across fresh-packed snow right into the curb. Cars honked and at least one driver waved hello with a single finger.

"What luck," I said. "There's time left on the meter."

From the outside, Mel's Cards and Comics didn't look like a child-friendly establishment, possibly because of the greasy windows and the location right next to an adult bookstore. Still, there were four kids inside when I entered. Ten A.M. on a Friday morning, why weren't they in school? For that matter, why wasn't I?

I dropped my keys on the glass-topped counter, and a woman behind the register smiled and held up a hand to silence me, then kept on counting bills and change. Finally, she closed the register drawer with a slam and smiled broadly. "Help you?"

I nodded and placed a flyer on the counter. "I'm

wondering if this guy ever came in and sold some baseball cards, maybe about a month ago."

She held it in both hands and leaned on her elbows. Made soft clucking noises as she studied it.

You don't have to memorize it, I thought. "Well?" I said.

"Not a real good picture of Scotty, is it? Oh, I was so sorry to hear about him dying."

"You know him?"

"Knew him, yeah. Regular. He was in three, four times a month to pick up the comics I'd hold for him. Maybe he'd buy or trade a couple of cards. Shoot the breeze about things. Sweet guy; changed my wiper blades for me once." She absently fingered the tiny gold cross hanging on a chain on her neck. "Who are you?"

"His sister."

Her jaw dropped and stayed in place until a little bead of saliva formed at the corner. "I never knew he had one."

"When did he last sell some cards to you?"

"Late December, maybe. He came in around then and had me look over his whole collection. Said he was thinking about giving them to a little girl he knew."

Hannah. "December, you sure?" Before the crash.

"Uh-huh."

"Did you buy any from him?"

"One. Made an offer on a few others, but he wasn't interested." A little boy pushed me aside and dropped a pile of change on the counter as he showed the woman the comic he was buying. She rang the sale and gave him a nickel change. "There weren't many high-end cards in his collection, one or two worth maybe seventy, eighty dollars. The others were nickel-and-dime stuff. Nothing to retire on, I told him, may as well give it to the little girl."

She looked again at the flyer. "Missing, you say? Not dead?"

"Yes. Just missing."

I hadn't even pulled into the driveway before Kady was hustling across the street after me. Early afternoon, she should have been in school. I could see her mother standing in the picture window, but it was impossible to see her expression at that distance. I was pretty sure I didn't want to. No doubt it would be murderously angry.

"Why aren't you in school?" I said. "Why isn't your mother at work?"

"Why aren't *you* in school?"

"Did your mother get you out to look for me?"

"Arden, the world does not revolve around you. Has it ever occurred to you that other people have problems?"

"Gosh, no. Thought I was the only one."

"My grandmother died this morning. Her heart failed. We're going back to Green Bay. We were just waiting for you to show up. The school said you called in sick. No one had any idea where you were." She was at that pinpoint place between rage and grief; I'd been there myself. Rage won and she reached out and banged her fist on my shoulder. "I don't care any more if you mess up your own life. I don't care if you flunk out of school and destroy your business and alienate your friends, but don't you dare screw around with my mother."

"I'm sorry."

"Don't say it if you don't mean it."

"I do mean it."

"Tell her you're sorry."

Mrs. Drummond looked like an older version of Kady, bearing the same combination of grief and rage. "I'm sorry about your mom," I said immediately. "And I'm sorry about skipping school this morning. Please . . ." I gave up. She wasn't really listening, and explaining wouldn't help.

Jean and her father left to load suitcases. "How soon can you be packed?" Mrs. Drummond said.

"Packed?"

"You're coming with us. Your winter break is next week and I don't feel right about leaving you alone for all that time."

"I have plenty to do. If I stay, I'll catch up on schoolwork, and maybe even get back to business. I have tons of frame orders. Oh, Mrs. Drummond, I am so sorry about your mother and sorry you have to worry about me, but I don't want to go."

Kady left us alone, exiting the room with a quick, angry step.

"Please," I said.

Mrs. D. looked out the window, toward my house. "My mother was eighty-two. How old was your mother when she died?"

"Forty-three."

"So young. You hadn't lived here that long and I'd hardly gotten to know them. I remember seeing Elizabeth planting tulip bulbs by flashlight the night before they left that last time. It was October, wasn't it? Yes, must have been. I guess she was afraid it would be too late when she returned from Honduras."

Never had returned, of course. "What a funny image," I said softly. "I'm glad you told me. I don't remember much."

"So young," she said again. She turned and hugged me. "No boys in the house. No parties. Get your work done. I want you to call me every night, no exception. And should Cody Rock or anyone try to get in, you call Al immediately. People want to help you; let them; it's a sign of good judgment."

"I'm sure it is. I promise to do everything right."

"One infraction and it's all over, and you come to live with us."

"I'll be fine. I'll be good, really really good. Thank you. I haven't said it before, but thank you for everything, Mrs. D."

She sort of melted then, and the tears slid out. Kady materialized and hugged her.

I turned around and faced the window and my empty house. A horrible thought crashed through: Would it have been so easy for Scott to leave if I'd ever said that to him? Just once, couldn't I have done it even one time? Looked him straight in the eye and said, Thank you.

14

"This is for me?" No doubt about it, Hannah was an all-round gorgeous child, but it was her eyes that would be heartbreakers. They were wide and bright as she leafed through the card album.

"You and the baby." Yeeps, what if she didn't know? I sneaked a peak at Claire, who didn't look especially perturbed.

Hannah carefully closed the album. "What if the baby doesn't like sports cards? Can I have them all?"

"Sure."

"But then you'll have to give the baby something to make it fair. Something that belonged to Scott, like the cards."

"You're right."

"Something that was special to him like these," Hannah said firmly. "Scott's the dad, you know."

Now I could see that Claire was upset, twisting in discomfort as her flesh and blood negotiated on behalf of the unborn sibling.

"When she turns sixteen she can have his car," I said.

Hannah's jaw dropped.

"It's a Plymouth Barracuda, kind of old, but in perfect shape. Best of all, it's a convertible. You and I will have to take care of it, though, so it still works when she's old enough to drive."

"I will," she said solemnly. She mumbled something about going to bed early, then picked up the album and went to her room.

"She'll be up all night memorizing every card and checking its value in one of her collectors' magazines," Claire said.

"They're never worth as much as you might hope," I said, thinking back to my trip to Mel's.

"It's still a sweet gift. No way, though, are you unloading that grotesque car on my children. I certainly won't thank you for that offer, but I will thank you for the pizza and the salad and the beautiful frame."

"Thank you for letting me invite myself over."

"We're being very polite, aren't we?"

"Very civil. It occurred to me that I owed you a huge apology, and it also occurred to me that I'd like to know this baby you're having. My niece or nephew. Hannah seems sure it's a girl. Do you know?"

Claire shook her head and turned to the sink to squeeze out a washcloth. She wiped down the counter without speaking, making long, wide strokes across the worn Formica.

It was a small kitchen, bright and warm but crowded with the appliances, chairs, and table. Staff housing for park employees wasn't spacious or luxurious, only four furnished rooms on the second floor of a duplex, spitting distance behind the park lodge.

"How are you feeling?"

"Pretty good. The fatigue is gone, and I never had much nausea." She ran water and rinsed the cloth. "Tea?"

"Yes, thank you."

"Not a very lively Saturday night for you, but then I suppose you can't throw a party every week."

"What exactly have you heard?"

She smiled. "There's quite a grapevine in this town."

"It reaches out here to the park?"

"Al keeps me posted."

"I bet. I haven't seen him much lately. Does he still come out to search the river?"

"Not as often. Once a week. He was here yesterday with his new girlfriend."

"He dumped the bank teller from Ashland? Scott would be pleased. I know he never liked her and was always trying to fix Al up with someone else."

Claire set mugs and tea bags on the counter. "In a way he did. She's the woman who owns the search dog." She picked up the whistling kettle. "Maybe she and Al will live happily ever after. That would be one good thing about Scott's death."

"Disappearance, Claire. Not death."

She slammed the kettle down on the red-hot range coil. Boiling water splashed out of the spout and splattered across her hand. She waved the burned hand in the air, then quickly turned on the cold-water faucet. "Arden," she said, her back turned to me as she ran water over the scald. "How do you think that makes me feel? How do you think I feel about someday telling my child that her father was so upset about the fact of her existence that he pretended to kill himself?"

I rose and took over making our tea. She'd picked peppermint. I sniffed the tea bags, inhaling the sweetness. I poured water into the mugs. "Has John talked to you about the estate, about how the baby would get Scott's money if he were dead?"

Her head moved slightly.

"I'll take that as a yes. Claire, I'm not doing this to hamper the baby getting what should be hers. If he was dead, I'd be the first one to hand over everything."

"I am not looking for money," she said tersely. "I don't care about his money. Let's not talk about money."

I set the kettle back on the range. "Tell me about the last few times you saw him."

"Because you care, or because you're putting together some puzzle?"

"I'd like to know more about my brother."

She tipped her head slightly to acknowledge the point. "We spent most of our time together talking."

Sure they did. I sucked down a smile and studied the steeping tea. And that's how you got pregnant, nature lady.

"He talked about you," she said. "Your business, your grades—"

"Uh-oh."

"He thought you and Hannah were a lot alike. When you were her age, that is. He was pretty certain you two would hit it off. Of course, he didn't exactly rush to have us all meet, did he?" She fingered a brass button on her sweater, then laid her hands on her belly. "He got a little down sometimes. Said once it would have been easier for you if you'd had an older sister around instead of him."

"That's absurd. And if he was so concerned, why

didn't he ever bring one home? He never introduced his dates."

She sipped tea, wiped her mouth with the back of her hand. "He talked about that, maybe just a few days before he died."

I shifted and raised an eyebrow. She shrugged. "Okay, before he plunged into the unknown."

"Better."

"He said he always worried about you being disappointed. That if you got attached to her and then they broke up, it would be hard on you. Actually, his exact words . . ." She smiled and shook her head.

"His exact words were what?"

"He said, 'The instant Arden sniffs a family, she'll go after it like a dog in heat.' "

"Idiot. Like he knew me."

"He didn't seem to worry about Hannah getting attached to him and then being disappointed. She liked him. She was always dragging him into the lodge so she could show off what she knew about the exhibits."

Poor Scott. The park lodge was a traditional Penokee elementary-school field trip destination. I didn't imagine that the stuffed animals and birds, the Touch Me displays of bones, fur, feathers, and snakeskins had provided a very romantic setting.

"One day, about a week after his first accident, I tried to teach him to snowshoe."

I spun around from the counter, mug in hand, and hot tea splashed on my wrist. "You did? Snowshoe? I never knew he could. Claire—that's wonderful, that's so important. If he asked you to teach him, don't you see that he was thinking about how he could get from the river to the road?"

"Whoa, Arden. What?"

"He must have asked you to let him try the shoes because he was planning to use them that day to get away from the river."

She took the mug out of my hand. "This for me?" I nodded. "Nice try, Arden." She sipped and shook her head when the hot water reached her tongue. "I forced him to try snowshoeing. And it didn't go at all well. After ten minutes he was red and huffing and puffing. Hannah was pretty merciless to him; she runs like a rabbit on hers." Claire cradled her mug and smiled. "I loved him for many reasons, but not his athleticism. If Scott actually snowshoed from the river to any spot on that road, then he must have been really determined to get the hell out." She lifted the mug. "Go, Scotty—you son of a bitch."

I sat at the table with my tea. "When I find him I plan to kill him, you know."

She let loose little deep rolls of laughter. "No. Don't."

"Oh, yeah. I miss the guy, but I'm totally pissed."

"What I meant was, should this little grief-induced fantasy prove true, and should you ever find him, please just hold him until I get there. We'll kill him together."

When I got back to the house I made my obligatory call to the Drummonds in Green Bay. Jean told me about their long day and I reported on my dinner with Claire.

"Talk to you tomorrow," I said. "Be good and kiss your mother."

I'd spent the afternoon cleaning the kitchen, getting groceries, and running other errands; then I'd gone to Claire and Hannah's. I hadn't checked the mail, which I usually did faithfully. I half expected to get a postcard from my brother. Someday, if I hadn't found him first, I felt sure I'd check the box and, stuck between a couple of magazines, there'd be a small rectangle with a gaudy scene of some tropical resort. "Alive and well, it was all a joke, home soon, lots to tell, love, Scott."

No postcard, but there was something else almost as nice: Jace had finally sent me the morphed picture of Scott.

It was so creepy—a face that wasn't his, but was. The clean-shaven face I hadn't seen in years. And maybe never would again.

Jace had included a short note. Two sentences, the eloquent male.

I think the picture's pretty good. Aren't computers wonderful?

Aren't computers wonderful?

Once again, illumination.

As I hit the computer power switch and listened to the machine boot up, I hoped I wouldn't find anything too embarrassing. Of course, I'd already gone through his drawers and pockets, so what was one more intrusion on a private place?

First I scanned his neatly organized and labeled folders. DESIGNS—those were elaborate, futuristic cars he'd created. DRAWINGS—just what it said. No bucolic landscapes, though; my brother was into drawing detailed fantasy figures. BOOKS AND MOVIES—that was a long list of titles. He'd gotten around to viewing and reading some of them, and he'd included the dates and brief comments.

Scott's organization was even more compulsive with his e-mail. He subscribed to two Internet mailing lists, and each week he'd made a new folder and tucked away all the messages worth keeping. Each week! Was that anal or what? Most of it was car nonsense. Good for something, though: I made a mental note to get the oil changed on my Honda.

I figured he probably had lots of new mail waiting, and I signed on to pull it down. His password? Ah, yes. BigTool. Macho man.

The new posts and messages he'd never seen were just as boring as the stuff he'd filed, and it reminded me why I had quit the lists I'd found for crafters: too many irritating digressions into weirdness. I pretty quickly realized I could skim the stuff from the lists because there was no way he'd have announced to people all over the world his intention to skip. There were a number of off-list messages, though. Evidently my brother had established close, personal relationships with other mechanics and 'Cuda fans around the world.

From Ebody@chip.link.com: *Scott, I'm planning to go to the swap meet in St. Paul. Good hotels?*

Hemiwhore@nevada.tech.edu: *I got the grill! Thanks for the lead.*

Oilchange@liverpool.com: *No! I see Dickens behind the wheel of one of your big dull American cars. Oldsmobile 88, perhaps?*

Doc460@whip.tech.edu: *Three words: Walt Whitman, Mazda Miata. Damn, that's four.*

Cars of the dead authors. Man, these mechanics had fun.

Those brought me up to New Year's. I rubbed my eyes, massaged my mouse hand, fixed some cocoa, and went back to work.

The late-January messages grew serious and for three days had settled on a single thread: Claire's pregnancy. Condolences, congratulations, advice, reproval, even crude jokes—everyone he'd met on the Internet had something to say.

I tipped the desk chair back and swiveled away from the computer. So he'd poured out his heart to a group of faceless strangers. Not to me, or Al, or John. After twelve years of carving out a life in Penokee, my brother had turned away from the people he knew and decided these cyberpals were the best friends he had.

No wonder it was so easy for him to leave: His life here meant nothing to him, his people meant nothing to him. Why hadn't I seen it, why had I been so absorbed in my own glorious world that I never once realized he hated his?

How ya doing, Scott? Whatcha thinking, brother? Tell me: What would *you* like?

I slapped the mouse and it skidded across the desk, hit the keyboard, and bounced up, then landed on a key. A new message clicked into view. It was from a verbose guy I'd figured out was a long-winded racist woman-hater, certainly not one of the mechanics interested in making literary connections to auto repair. I hated his posts, and after the one where he blasted Claire for "trapping" Scott, I skimmed them all. I scanned this one and almost hit NEXT before the message registered.

I know the feeling, Scott. Boxed in, right? You said you wanted to jump—just let me know when you're ready. I'm here.

Bingo. Bull's-eye. Home run.

The message was dated two days after the disappearance. That meant this guy, Overdrive@thunderlink.com, hadn't helped plan the escape, but he must have known something about what Scott was thinking or feeling.

Boxed in. What exactly had my brother told this guy that he'd never said to me?

I'm here for you. Well, where was "here"?

I checked the remainder of the mail quickly and found nothing special, unless silence from Overdrive was significant. He'd never written Scott again. Because my boxed-in brother came knocking at his door begging for help? I spent another half hour going back over all of Overdrive's messages to the mech list, trying to cull a clue as to where he lived. I could have simply shot him a message and asked him straight out, but if he was hiding Scott, it would have been a signal that someone was looking.

Around midnight I found the answer filed in the previous year's March 1–7 folder. From Overdrive: *Good news! For the second time the main shop has won the Northern Ontario Ad Council's best print campaign. My gorgeous mug and studlike body (joke, mates) have become the symbol for Pete's Body Shop. Can't go into a restaurant in Thunder Bay without being recognized. Embarrasses the hell out of Pete Junior, especially when it's a lady giving me the once-over. But then he's only sixteen and no way he's going to admit I've still got it.*

Oh, Pete in Thunder Bay. Just what is it you've got? My brother?

"Is Pete there?"

All day Sunday I had planned for this moment. Might say I obsessed. I talked to Pete while I cleaned the kitchen, I typed *Pete* twice in the same sentence while working on an English paper, I said "Hello, Pete" when Mr. Drummond answered the phone in Green Bay. I figured if this Pete knew anything at all, I would sense it immediately, even if we weren't face-to-face. There'd be a hesitation, or some cheery bluster, or maybe he'd blurt one of the favorite words that peppered his posts.

Why did he feel boxed in, Pete? What did he say he was going to do about it, Pete? Where do you suppose he is, Pete? Why did he confide in *you*, Pete?

"Sorry, miss, Pete isn't here."

I squeezed the phone. I hadn't prepared for that.

"Will he be back soon?" In the background I heard the familiar loud noises of a garage.

"Not until Thursday. He went to the shoe shop."

Four days to buy shoes? "Shoe shop?"

"*Soo* shop," he shouted. "Went to Sault Ste. Marie, to one of his other garages. Harbor View Auto. Like I said, back on Thursday."

But I want an answer now, mister. "Could I reach him there?"

"What's this about, miss?"

Think fast, Arden. My missing brother? No good—that would set off alarms even before I talked to Pete. "His son."

"Not in trouble again, is he?"

"I'm a friend from school. Peter said his father might look over a car for me."

"Well, like I said, he'll be in Sault this week. Starting a new guy."

"He's what?" My voice spun down an octave as my heart flew up into my mouth.

"Starting a new mechanic at the shop, another muscle-and-vintage guy. Don't know why they need two there when we could use one here, but I'm not the boss."

"Thank you, sir. Thank you very much."

Muscle-and-vintage guy—perhaps a 'Cuda specialist? I hadn't believed it would be so easy. One phone call and I'd found him.

Almost found him. No way I was going to make the final snare over the phone.

I had long-term goals: high-school graduation, college, travel, become an obnoxiously doting aunt. All in good time. But just then, the only thing I wanted to do was walk into Pete's Harbor View Auto and drop a net over my brother's bald head. Gotcha.

16

In eighth grade I had a student teacher in social studies who was really into geology. She'd bring in rocks and we were supposed to marvel at them.

"Precambrian!" she exclaimed once, holding up a nondescript chunk that looked like it had been lifted out of someone's backyard landscaping. "From right here in Wisconsin. Does anyone know what *Precambrian* means?"

Possibly some of us did, but her enthusiasm dampened our flickering interest. No one spoke.

"Very, very old," she said patiently. "Only the humblest forms of plant or animal life had appeared. This rock is over a billion years old."

I knew there were at least a half dozen kids in class who didn't believe in evolution and would be ready to stare her down and rattle off a theory of creationism. But I suspected they were thinking the same thing I was: Fresh teacher, don't bother, she'll burn out soon enough.

She did. By the end of her eight-week stint she'd given up on show-and-tell and was simply assigning text pages to read and giving multiple-choice tests. She must have left something with me, though. As I drove across Wisconsin and then Michigan's snow-covered Upper Peninsula, through the Porcupine Mountains, and across the flats down toward Sault and Canada, I couldn't help thinking about the origins of the area—how it resulted from the combination of glaciers and volcanoes. Cold and hot, pretty much how I felt about my brother. Bone-chilling grief and fiery rage. Ice and fire.

Seven hours after I'd talked to the guy in Thunder Bay I was at the international border, crossing from Sault Ste. Marie, Michigan, to Sault St. Marie, Ontario. You'd think they might have tried harder with the names. I was the only car going over the bridge, so maybe boredom was the reason the guy took a long time to check my ID and car papers.

"The reason for your visit?" he asked

"Visiting relatives." Bit of a stretch, of course.

"School holiday?" he asked.

"Yes, sir," I said truthfully.

He waved me through and I cruised slowly. I didn't have a clue as to where I should go, I didn't even know if I needed to drive on the wrong side of the road. I pulled over, parked, looked around. My first time ever in a foreign country, though I don't know if most people think of Canada that way. I guess visiting there is sort of like Travel for Beginners.

I stopped at a service station, got directions from the clerk, then found the garage with only two wrong turns. The shop should never have been called Harbor View. It was a sprawling mud-brown building on a busy commercial street far from the water. I parked and watched the entrance. The wide service door rolled up and a blue pickup drove out. The door rolled down. It was growing dark, the end of the workday. I watched three more vehicles leave. Each time the door dropped, my hopes sank further. He wasn't there. I knew that from just watching the shop and feeling the rumble of the truck traffic on the street. Scott ran away for this? All I could see was a cold, wintry port city. Duluth or Superior, with even less charm.

Leave no stone unturned, though. I got out and jogged across the street. An older woman was approaching the shop and I waited while she opened the door; then I followed her in. The receptionist smiled, but only at the woman. She seemed to assume we were together. Fine. I looked down a hall past the counter, saw a door marked GARAGE—EMPLOYEES ONLY. I checked over my shoulder and saw the two women discussing a bill. I slipped down the hall, peeked through the window on the garage door, saw a head approach, then spun around and bent down to get a drink at the fountain. Spat it out. Warm water.

The garage door swung open and a small man with gray hair came out. No mechanic's overalls, just a tweed sport coat, shirt, tie. Pete the Boss? I let him get a few steps away; then I slipped through the door. My jacket pocket snagged on the doorknob and I twisted around to release it.

"You lost, angel?"

I looked up. Half a dozen mechanics in dark blue coveralls were crowded around a suit holding a clipboard.

"What can we do for you?" the suit said.

"Nothing. Just checking on the car for my mother."

"Name?"

Aw, geez. "Never mind, I see it, looks like it's almost done."

The suit turned to the man on his left. "And in case we haven't loaded you with enough the last couple of days, Rooney, here's another rule to memorize: no customers in the shop. The boss got sued once when some idiot barged in and slipped on something and cut a pinkie." He eyed me. "Employees only, no exceptions."

Rooney, the new boy, nodded eagerly, then turned to me and imitated the suit's glare. I took a last look at his long lean body, the yellow-toothed sneer, his greasy blond ponytail. I'd driven seven hours to check out the new guy at Harbor Auto and now I'd seen him. An oaf.

Back in the hallway I was bumped by the gray-haired guy as he rushed from an office. We both apologized; then he disappeared into the men's room. I glanced into the office.

"Oh, man," I muttered.

The walls were covered with photographs of sky divers. Solo jumpers, duos, circles of eight holding hands.

Let me know when you're ready to jump.

Pete Senior hadn't been offering my brother escape and a new life, just the chance to leap into the sky.

The clerk at the Super Sleep Motel turned my ArdenArt Visa over several times, as if he was looking for fine print that said "Yes, just as you suspect, this is a fake."

"I have a small business," I said. "Craft items. I'm in town visiting vendors."

"Uh-huh. May I see an ID?"

I was ready with my license. Not a great picture, but good enough. The clerk held the two cards side by side, then shrugged and let me register.

I used my ArdenArt phone card to call the Drummonds as soon as I was in the room. John, I hoped, wouldn't scrutinize my business bills as closely as my personal ones. A call from Wild-Goose Chase, Michigan, would look mighty suspicious.

Mrs. Drummond answered. She sounded pretty wiped—no surprise, considering she'd buried her mother that afternoon. I tried to sound cheerful. Yes, I was fine, I murmured. Yes, it snowed a bit. Did the funeral go okay? Oh, what did I do today, you ask? Studied, worked in the shop, shoveled. Good night and good-bye.

I bounced on the soft mattress of the double bed in a cheap motel in Michigan and wondered when I had gotten so good at lying.

17

I did shovel when I got home. Cleared my walk and drive, then worked on the Drummonds'. There'd been only a few inches and it didn't seem worthwhile to fire up the snowblower, so I did it the old-fashioned way. An hour later my muscles were screaming. This should not have surprised me, considering that the most strenuous exercise I usually enjoyed was lifting and lowering a hammer—and I hadn't done even that for weeks.

While Scott's tub was filling, I called Jace. "Is it important?" his mother asked. "He's been running a fever all day and he's resting."

I politely assured her that it was. "You don't sound feverish," I said as soon as he answered. "Faking, I bet. Did you get to ditch school, or are you on break, too? I hope so, because today I got this other idea and I have something else I want you to do. I was thinking we should get copies of the color picture you made and take them around to travel agents. You kept one, didn't you? I could send you some, but it would be faster if you could run off a few more on your own and then take them around to the travel agencies in Duluth. I'd pay you for the copies."

"So you did get the picture."

"Didn't I thank you? It was great, kind of weird to look at, though. Have you had a chance to check the mailbox rentals and the car lots? I need that, Jace; I feel like time is running out." I used my foot to nudge the tub faucet off. The flow of water sputtered to a halt. "You would not believe where I've been." I gave him a quick recap of my Canadian trip, skipping the geology lesson.

He didn't say anything when I finished. "Have you ever been to Sault Ste. Marie?" I prompted.

"Arden," he said slowly, "my mom's not real happy about all these assignments you're giving me. She knows the deputy who was in charge of the search, and well, they've talked and everything, and now Mom doesn't think it's such a good idea for me to be taking the car and driving around hunting for your brother."

"What do *you* think?"

"It's kind of a lot to do—sports stores, mailbox rentals, now travel agents."

"I need help, Jace."

"I'd like to, but . . . Arden, it was really nice seeing you and spending that day together. I wish we lived closer. I mean, I could even see working out a long-distance, um, thing. I guess what I mean is I'd be happy to be your boyfriend, but I'm not wild about being your assistant. And it seems like that's what you want from me."

"I don't think of you that way."

"I'm not sure you think of me at all, except to give orders. I don't want to be too rude or anything, but would it hurt you to say 'How are you?' before you say 'Do this'?"

Even in the steamy bathroom, I could feel the chill. "I'm sorry you feel that way. I've been preoccupied, I know, but it's important."

"I know that, Arden, and I know I'm sort of being a jerk, considering it's been a pretty bad winter for you and all, but if the only thing you want from me is someone to play detective, well, I'm out. By the way, I got a part in the play. Thanks for asking."

I let a silence build a bit, then thanked him—sweetly—and hung up. Not much more to say after that, why pretend?

I lowered myself into the bathwater. It was almost unbearably hot, but not nearly as scathing as Jace's kiss-off. Well, since he'd already scalded me, why not get parboiled?

I sank into the water until it lapped at my ears. A long-distance *thing*, he'd called it. Maybe he was right—what was the future in that? No big loss.

The phone rang while I was drying and the machine obediently kicked in. Maybe Jace had had second thoughts and was calling to apologize. I heard Hannah's voice, but not what she was saying. Another get-lost message, no doubt.

Later I made some toast and listened to her funny rundown of the prices of the cards I'd given her. I checked my watch. Not too late, I could still give her a call. Okay, she wasn't an attractive guy with a gentle kiss, but if a six-year-old was the best I could do for an admirer, I'd settle. Just as I picked up the portable to call her back, the doorbell rang. I wasn't dressed, of course. People never dropped in when I was dressed. By the time I reached the front door, the visitor had given up on the bell and started knocking, louder and louder. My hand froze on the knob.

"We know you're there, so let us in." Cody and friends. "C'mon, Arden, we'll be good this time." The pounding grew harder. "We see the lights. Open up." There was some murmuring, a mix of male and female voices. Then: "Go see if she left the back door open."

Had I locked it when I came in? I wheeled around and looked across the living room to the brightly lit kitchen. The blind over the window was open and anyone walking by could look in and see me standing there. I dropped down to the floor, out of view, and sat with my back against the door. Someone opened the storm door and pounded hard enough to bounce my shoulders.

"Oh, Arrrr-den," Cody called. "We know you're there!"

There was banging on the back door, and someone had a finger glued to that bell. It had a high tinny ring. Cody heard it and started ringing the front bell to answer.

Real funny, ha ha. The bell ringers pressed faster and harder: front, one-two-three, pause; back, one-two-three; pause. The ringing smeared into screeching.

I pulled up my knees and the cordless phone fell out of my hand.

People want to help you; let them; it's a sign of good judgment.

I picked up the phone, rose, and unlocked the door.

Cody and cohorts stood on the stoop.

"Knew we'd get you. C'mon, Arden—let's just have some fun. We promise—"

I held up the phone. "Watch this, you bastard," I said, and punched in 911.

"This is Arden Munro at Forty Riverview Drive," I told the dispatcher. "I have prowlers."

18

"John, I need help."

I'd caught him eating lunch. He'd tucked his tie into his shirt while he ate soup at his desk. He wiped his chin with a napkin, then sipped from a bottle of water.

"Why aren't you in school? And don't ask me to lie about it if the principal calls."

"Winter break."

"What do you want?"

"Some of my money. Mrs. Drummond will be home tomorrow and you can talk about it with her then, but I'm sure if you say it's okay, she'll agree. And if you let me have what I need, when it's gone I promise to stop. Completely."

"You make about as much sense as these suit papers I've been reading." He tapped a file on his desk with his thumb. "Ten-year-old kid gets hurt falling off an ATV at his cousin's, now all the aunts and uncles are suing each other. Georgetown Law School, and this is what I do. What do you need the money for?"

"I want to hire a detective."

"I prefer the term *investigator*," Rose Vanaci said. She slipped a thumb under the neckline of her dress and adjusted a bra strap. "*Detective* is a police title."

Her secretary knocked and poked her head in. "Milwaukee coroner's office on line two." Rose shrugged an apology, then picked up her phone. I gave her some privacy by turning my head and looking out the window. I could see my car parked across the street, just in front of the Superior Bar and Grill. A UPS truck blew down the street and covered my windshield with a back spray of brown-sugar snow.

"So you want me to find your brother?"

I faced her and smiled. "Yes. John Abrahms called you, right?"

"He did. He also told me that you are the only one in the world who believes your brother is alive."

"There are two in the world who *know* he's alive: my brother and me."

"I won't argue the point. Let's begin by assuming you're right."

I sighed and relaxed in the chair. Okay, even if I had reached the point where I had to pay someone to agree with me, it still felt good to hear: *You're right*. "Thank you, Ms. Vanaci."

"Rose, please. You'll be spilling all the family secrets to me, so we may as well forget formalities. Now, the first thing I need to know is why you want to find him. By leaving, he's shown he doesn't want you in his life. That's harsh, of course, but it's my role to probe in some tender spots. From what John has told me I understand you have the means and spirit to succeed on your own, Arden, so why pursue him? Why do you want him back?"

"Not sure I do anymore, exactly," I said slowly, understanding my feelings only as I chose my words. "But I do want to show everyone that they were wrong and I was right; I want apologies from everyone." She had a tray of paper clips on her desk. I picked one up and bent it open. "It wasn't such a great life he had, taking care of me, and I understand how maybe he felt smothered. I wish I'd figured that out earlier and said something; maybe he wouldn't have gone. But even though I know it's partly my fault that he hated his life, I'm still mad that he jerked us around this way. I want to jerk him back. It's all mixed up, I guess. One minute I feel sorry for him, then the next I want to kill him."

"Honest reasons, but mostly negative ones."

"Okay, here's a good reason: You bring him back, and right before I kill him, I plan to say, 'Thank you for my life.' Better?"

She smiled. "Good enough. John told me there's no sign of missing money."

"Seems that way."

"That makes it easier for us. A person can't go far or hide deep with no money. If you're willing to just wait it out, he'll probably show up on his own."

"I want to find him."

"Ooh, that's a murderous look. I've seen it often."

"Do you do a lot of this?"

"Missing persons are my specialty. Most of my cases are domestic—moms or dads who've snatched their own kids."

"Were you a cop?"

"Fifteen years, Milwaukee Police. Then I put in seven as a fraud investigator for an insurance company. Now I'm my own man."

Not a man at all, of course, and certainly not what I'd expected. I'd climbed the steps to her second-floor office overlooking the busiest street in Superior expecting to enter a dark, smoky office. Even the name was right: Rose Vanaci—sounded like a tough broad. Instead I found a tastefully decorated suite of rooms and a middle-aged woman groomed for an appearance on the pages of some upscale magazine. Perfectly frosted hair, tailored mauve silk dress, subtle makeup. She even had disarming family pics on the wall. Husband, two kids, grandchildren. Ugly frames, though.

"John said you'd done a little searching on your own. What have you done?"

My efforts seemed pretty pathetic now. "I put up missing-guy posters, ran an ad locally, checked a few car and mailbox rentals, snooped through his drawers and computer files."

"And found . . . ?"

"Nothing. No dirty pictures, no leather underwear, no secret life. Even the computer folders were cleaned up. There was nothing except a hint that he was interested in taking up skydiving. What will *you* do to find him?"

"Pretty much what you've been doing, but I'll use a wider net. I'll make a lot of phone calls and fax out a lot of pictures. I'll contact motor vehicle departments and I'll buy lots of mailing lists to look for new subscribers fitting his profile. If he's alive I'll find him, and chances are I'll never leave my office."

"Never?"

"Well, I'll go home at night and play wife and grandmother. Do you have a picture of your brother?"

I handed her the flyer and Jace's morphed photo. "Before and after shaving. The flyer photo is real. The other one was done on a computer to show what he'd look like without a beard. A friend did it for me. I think it's probably pretty good."

"It's wonderful. Could be very helpful. Now, I need one more thing from you."

"Yes?"

"Tell me everything about yourself and Scott and your parents."

"But that's another reason I want to find him. I don't know everything. At times, I feel like I don't know anything at all."

"Three thousand bucks?" Kady dropped her spoon and stared. "They're letting you spend that much money on a detective?"

"She prefers to be called an investigator. You have yogurt on your chin."

"And my mother agreed to this?"

"Yup. There's a time limit and a money limit, but she and John agreed. I'm surprised she didn't tell you."

"Stuff about being your guardian she thinks is confidential. I had no idea. Three thousand. I've been going to every civic group in the county begging on my knees for scholarship money and you're spending three grand to find a corpse. Why don't you just burn it? Or give it away to one of these jerks." She lifted her arm and motioned behind her, where most of the cafeteria population was looking in our direction.

Cody saw me, sneered, bit down on a sandwich.

"Most everyone in this room would blow it on a party," I said.

"Three thousand," she whispered. Stunned.

We had a sixth-hour pep fest to kick off the start of hockey playoffs. The Penokee Panthers went 9–12 during the regular season, but they'd won their last eight straight and the gym was raucous with hopeful fans. Kady was student council president and usually led the pep talks, but today she turned it over to one of the players and took a chair onstage by the team. While he gave a funny talk about Penokee's hockey tradition, she looked over the audience until she found me. She stared.

I waved and made a face. She didn't respond, didn't even look away. Easy to read her mind: Three thousand bucks.

We were dismissed from the assembly and I went straight to the library for study hall. I was nearly caught up on missing assignments and had even started reading history again. More accurately, I was reading it for the first time. Maybe, just maybe, if I was caught up and promised to be a good girl, Ms. Penny would let me rejoin her class and I could avoid summer school, an earthly form of hell if there ever was one.

I was hunched over a table with eyes glued to a text when Kady entered the library, paused by my table, then went to one of the computers. I watched as she logged on to the Internet server and started typing. After a couple of minutes I got bored and returned to the fascinating facts about royal marriage patterns in nineteenth-century Europe.

I was packing my bag when the bell rang. Kady stood at the printer, waiting as it churned out a few pages. She placed them in a folder and put that into her backpack.

"Want a ride home?" It was routine, of course, but I needed a safe subject for conversation.

"Thanks. Jean said to tell you she's staying late. Editorial deadline. I need to go to my locker. Meet you at the car."

Routine, again. But there was nothing ordinary about the papers she handed me as she got out when we reached my house. "What's this?" I asked.

"Just some stuff I found in the U medical library."

I frowned. We had full access to all University of Wisconsin libraries through school, but the medical library?

"At the risk of ruining our friendship, I've decided that I have to be the one who gets you to face facts."

"Facts?"

She wiped snow off the roof of the car with her coat sleeve. "Scott's dead." She nodded toward the folder I was holding. "That's what the investigator should be looking for. That's what he looks like." She turned and crossed the street toward home.

I closed the garage door and went in the house. I laid the folder on the kitchen counter and turned on the lights. I nudged up the temp on the thermostat and hung up my coat. I made a sandwich and poured some milk. I opened the folder, looked at the top sheet, and nearly lost all the food from a lifetime of overeating.

Dead bodies. My dear old friend, sweet responsible Kady, had searched the libraries of the university system until she had found a book full of pictures of dead bodies. A medical pathology text, three pages from chapter seven, "Drowning and the Body."

Bloated corpses, white waxy skin, empty eye sockets, missing parts.

I called the Drummonds, tapping the numbers in so

fast I got a wrong number. Tried again. She answered. "Obviously, I'm not the one who needs help," I said. "Did you have fun looking for these?"

"I just think—"

"I know what you think and I don't care. I'm doing what I want to do, so all you have to do is shut up and cope with it. If you don't, we just won't be friends." I hung up before she could respond to my threat. I crumpled the pictures and pitched them into the sink. My GPA, my business, Jace. Now I could chalk up one more loss to Scott's little adventure: a best friend.

20

"Arden, will you be my best friend?"

"I'm a little old for you."

Hannah spooned heated fudge topping over her bowl of ice cream. "That would only matter if you were my lover."

I sputtered, shooting drops of pop over the table.

"Hey!" she said, grabbing a handful of napkins, then handing them to me. "Clean it up."

What had I been like at age six? Was I saucy? Quiet? Could I read? Had I known the meaning of the word *lover*?

Hannah was sleeping over. My idea, and three hours into the experiment, it was working out just fine. We'd watched one movie, made and eaten a large sausage and onion pizza, and fixed dessert, and were about to watch the second of our three videos, *Meet Me in St. Louis*.

We were probably the only people in town that particular Friday night. The Panthers, after their mediocre season, had made it into the state hockey tourney. Even the Drummonds, school supporters but hardly hockey fans, had traveled to Madison for the tournament.

"First and probably the only time," Jean had said. "You've got to come with us."

"Alone again?" Mrs. Drummond frowned.

"You can look over the university campus," said Mr. D. "We'll check out the art department."

Kady said nothing. She and I had kept a cool distance since the day last week when she'd dumped the pictures on me. She waited, probably anticipating that her family would change its plans to accommodate my wishes.

"I've offered to take Hannah for the weekend," I said, thinking fast. "Claire needs the break."

True enough, though I'd only thought about making the offer and hadn't actually done so.

"A six-year-old?" said Jean. "Weird."

"How kind," said Mrs. Drummond.

"Bring her along," said Mr. D., probably hoping I wouldn't.

"Suit yourself," said Kady.

It suited me fine to be spending the weekend with a kid instead of cheering on the hometown team in the state's favorite blood sport. Lately I'd felt like I'd all but disappeared from high school. Oh, I showed up daily and I was even doing the best work in years. But that afternoon as I sat through the second pep fest in two weeks, I realized that the appeal of high-school life eluded me. The games, the rah-rah convocations, the raucous playfulness in the cafeteria—what a waste. More often than not I'd sit alone in the lunchroom, looking at the kids I'd known since first grade and wondering, Who *are* these people?

Yup, Hannah was plenty good company.

She added still more topping to her ice cream. I frowned. "You've used five different spoons so far."

"You don't want me to use them again after I licked. You said so. Should we get our pajamas on before we watch the movie?"

"Okay."

"I've got new ones. Mom made them."

"She sews?"

"Of course. They have baseballs and gloves on them. I get to stay the whole weekend, right?"

"Right." Which would mean about three more trips to the video store and at least one more run for groceries. I'd seriously underestimated the appetite of the child.

"If I don't have to go home until Sunday, can we go to the Mall of America tomorrow?"

"I can't."

"Why?"

Why indeed? After all, I'd driven to Canada on a whim. "I made a promise to someone that I wouldn't go anywhere without asking her. She's out of town until Sunday."

Hannah set down her spoon. "You have your own car and your own house and you need *permission*?"

"Yes."

She shook her head sorrowfully, and together, as we ate our sundaes, we contemplated the injustice.

I got permission.

"What a wonderful idea!" Mrs. Drummond said. "And how lovely that you and Hannah are getting so close."

"She's an okay kid," I said. "May I have more of that pot roast?"

Mr. Drummond handed the platter to me, passing it right across Kady, who didn't seem to notice the beef under her nose.

"Anyone want to come along?" I looked right at her. "Please?"

"Not me," said Jean, sitting across the table. "I intend to do some serious sleeping this weekend. Besides, I hate the place. Crass commercialism, the worst of America all under one roof. Noisy, expensive, crowded, artificial. Should I go on?"

"No, thanks," Kady said. "To both of you." She rose. "I set the table. Someone else can clean up." She left the room without having said a direct word to me the whole meal.

Well, I'd tried.

21

I was pink-slipped in algebra again. "Not another session with the shrink," I muttered.

"I've been so good and obedient, Mrs. Rutledge," I

blurted as soon as I entered her office. "I haven't put up a flyer in a couple of weeks, I haven't sneaked into Duluth, and I only call the detective every other day." Of course, I'd sabotaged a budding romance and a lifelong friendship, but she didn't have to know all that. She motioned me to a chair and closed the door.

Closed door, grim counselor. This was bad. "What's up?" I said.

"Al Walker called me. He and John Abrahms are on their way to— Oh, Arden, he asked me to pull you out of class and tell you personally. Some men were fishing close to where the Gogebic runs into Lake Superior. With all this warm weather we've had the past few days, the river is running hard, even under the ice cover."

"What are you saying? Where have John and Al gone?"

She twisted the rings on her left hand. "County morgue in Ashland. The fishermen found a body in the water."

She called Kady and Jean out of their classes to take me home. Jean shouldered my book bag and Kady handed me my jacket after removing the car keys from a pocket. "I'll drive," she said.

She not only drove but guided me out of the car and into her kitchen, made me tea, called her mother and father with the news, put together a plate of nutritious munchies, and left a message for Al at the police station that I could be reached at her house. Not once did she say, "I told you so."

The three of us sat together on the long davenport and waited for something. Kady on my right, Jean on the left, both turned toward me. I faced the wall across the room, looking at their family pictures, all arranged in a circle around a large photo of Mr. and Mrs. D. on their wedding day.

Jean reached under a cushion and pulled out three beanbags; they had practice gear stashed in every room. She tossed them a few times, then sent one over my head to her sister, who grabbed it with an angry slash and put it away. "Not now," Kady said sharply.

I folded my hands and spent a few minutes studying the neat way fingers fit together. Nothing neat about my nails, though. Fix-up time. Maybe a new color. Red? Pearl? Something glittery? Black might be suitable.

"I guess this is it," I said. My first words since leaving school.

"Yes," said Kady.

"At least we know what the body will look like, huh?"

"That was awful of me," said Kady. "I can't believe I did it."

"Did what?" asked Jean.

"You meant to be helpful," I said.

"I meant to shake you awake. I should have known it would happen soon enough."

"Am I included in this conversation?" Jean said.

"You didn't keep them, did you?"

"Keep what, or don't I get to know?" Jean said.

"I made a fire and burned them in the sink."

Jean held her hands in front of her face and turned them from side to side. "Gosh, I don't seem to be invisible."

Kady tossed the beanbag back, hitting her hard on the shoulder. "You don't want to know."

"Yes, I do. Arden, please tell?"

"I'll tell," Kady said. "I downloaded some pictures from a medical library and gave them to Arden. Drowned bodies."

Jean hugged an embroidered throw pillow. "That's sick."

"I just felt so frustrated, Arden, that you were ignoring the truth."

I nodded. "Can't ignore it now. So what do I do? I've never planned a funeral."

"Mom and Dad will help."

"Oh, girls," Jean said, "aren't we forgetting one small thing?"

"What?" I asked.

"No one has actually said the body was identified. What if it's not him?"

Al and John arrived while we were eating supper. No one had eaten much, probably because of the prevailing mood, or maybe it was the heavy dose of hot sauce Jean had mixed into the scrambled eggs.

I was first to the door after the bell rang. The guys stood there, tired and grim. I motioned them in. Who would speak first?

Al unzipped his jacket. "It wasn't Scott."

John walked in and nodded to the Drummonds, who had clustered behind me. He collapsed on a chair.

"Worst thing I've ever had to do. I've never been to the morgue before. God, Arden, I hope you're right. I hope he is alive. I hope he doesn't look like that. You have no idea."

Kady and I exchanged glances.

"Yes, she does," Jean muttered.

Some internal Betty Crocker alarm went off in Mrs. D. and she slipped away to the kitchen. Probably whipping up some nonspicy eggs for the guys.

"Who was it?" I asked.

"Don't know," said Al. "Someone who was in the water a lot longer than Scott. Couple of sea kayakers disappeared last summer. Maybe it was one of those guys."

"How did you know it wasn't Scott?" I asked.

"It was so battered," said John, more to himself than us. "There was nothing human about it. There wasn't even a face." The twins simultaneously crossed arms and flinched.

"This body was a male Caucasian," Al said to me, "and it washed up close to the mouth of the Gogebic, so the deputies up there right away thought of Scott. This person, though, was at least six feet tall. Lots of things happen to a corpse in water, but it doesn't grow six inches."

Hope was renewed, but it was hard not to think that the waiting would soon be over for someone else.

"Do I look wonderful?" Hannah spun around, modeling a new haircut and sweater. Her hand swiped across the table in their kitchen, sending a mug wobbling toward the edge. Her mother lunged and made the rescue.

"You do. Quite beautiful. Who made the sweater?"

"Mom. I picked the yarn. Can we go now? You've talked so long."

Claire and I exchanged smiles; I'd been in their kitchen for maybe five minutes.

"Words cannot express my gratitude," Claire said. "Ever since Scott mentioned to her that they might go to the Mall, she's been anxious. I went once, years ago, and have no desire to do so ever again. So I'm grateful, but I wish you'd let me pay for it."

"My treat, don't argue. It's you and me, kiddo," I said to Hannah. "I guess we're the only people in Penokee who know how to have fun."

"Mom doesn't. She's working. They're making bird feeders today."

I turned to Claire and raised my eyebrows.

"The last day of an Elderhostel. We're snowshoeing, bird watching, and then making feeders. Twenty senior citizens and me."

I grinned. "Good thing you've got that master's degree in biology."

"Don't wait up," Hannah shouted as she pushed open the door.

"Ha," I said. "We'll be home by eight."

Hannah waved an envelope in my face as I buckled my seat belt. "Look what I got," she said.

"I can't look because you'll poke my eyes out. Put that down. What is it?"

"I got a card from my dad yesterday. Last weekend I called him and told him we were going to the megamall today. That was before they found that body. I heard Mom talking to Al about it. If it was Scott's body would we be going?"

"Probably not."

"Then I'm glad it wasn't him. I heard Mom tell Grandma on the phone she wished it *was* him. She wished it was all over, she said."

I looked over my shoulder as we backed up onto the snow-packed road.

"Dad never writes letters. He's always too busy. He's a neur-o-surgeon." She said the long word carefully. "He lives in Phoenix. He sent this card. I got it yesterday." She pulled the card out and opened it. " 'Have fun, sweetheart,' " she read slowly.

"That's nice."

"There's something else," she said. She pulled out a bill and waved it in the air. "A hundred dollars."

I shifted and hit the gas. "Cool."

"Mom gets so mad when he sends me big money."

"She does?" Keep talking, kid. I want to know everything.

"We better not tell her, okay?"

"Okay."

"So let's spend it all."

. . .

It's not hard to blow a hundred bucks at the megamall. For starters, hitting all the rides three or four times makes a nice dent in the cash. It's the biggest mall in the country, maybe the world, and it was packed with Saturday shoppers, mostly pale Midwesterners needing an escape from the long winter. And as always, there were quite a few people who came from even farther away. I heard what I think was German, French, and Spanish and I saw plenty of Japanese couples, all of whom seemed to be on some sort of honeymoon special.

Lines moved slowly in Camp Snoopy, the indoor amusement park. We had long waits for the roller coaster and the other good rides. Hannah amused herself by working on a small handheld puzzle she'd bought at a toy store. I looked for bald heads. This wasn't a conscious act, just habit.

By midafternoon I was beat. Three roller-coaster rides, four log-chute drops, three Mystery Mine rides, and miles of walking had taken a toll. We found an empty bench on the third floor and collapsed. Hannah opened her wallet and counted. "Seven dollars and thirty-five cents."

I'd dropped forty, which isn't small change, but she'd spent over ninety-two dollars in a few hours. Was that some sort of a record? Probably not, but pretty good for a six-year-old.

"Better leave enough for a present for your mom," I advised.

A bald biker dude in head-to-toe black leather strolled by, carrying three bags from Victoria's Secret. Gifts, or for his own wardrobe? I laughed at the thought that maybe my brother had left home to go live like that guy.

"What's funny?" Hannah asked.

"Nothing."

She followed my gaze and noticed the biker. "You shouldn't laugh at people."

"Hannah," I said, putting my arm around her, "it's a good thing I like you. Otherwise, I'd think you were pretty obnoxious."

A mother of twin infants was getting frustrated trying to give her babies a snack as she sat on a narrow ledge around some fake greenery. I hauled Hannah up and signaled to the mother, letting her know she could have the bench. She moved over gratefully.

Hannah led me to the escalators and we rode down two levels. The cacophony of mall music, rattling roller coaster, and thousands of jabbering people made talking impossible. She window-shopped, I dragged along. "What are you doing?" she asked at one point when I stood still and she walked on, her hand slipping out of mine.

"Nothing, just looking," I said. Couldn't help it. Reflex, I guess. This was the busiest place I'd been to since he'd disappeared. Everywhere I turned, I saw guys who were the right height or had the same coloring. Guys alone, with friends, with children. For the millionth time since February, I wondered, Where is he? What is he doing? Is he alone?

Hannah tugged on my sleeve. "How many rides do we have left?" We cut through the stream of people to get to a ticket scanner. TEN POINTS, the display flashed as it read our ride card.

"Enough for one more each," I said.

She decided on the Mystery Mine again. We waited in line for twenty minutes, then enjoyed three minutes of spine-wrenching fun, strapped into rocking seats as we watched a stomach-dropping you-are-there movie about a ride through a mammoth mine.

The lights went on. We blinked, unbuckled the restraints, picked up our bags, and exited with the crowd. I felt Hannah's small hand hook on to my back pocket. Outside the theater in the crowded Camp Snoopy, her hand slipped off. I turned to find her and was jostled and pushed aside by a loud group of teenagers. "Hannah!" I called. I stood on tiptoes to look back into the crowd behind me.

Then I saw him.

Short, strong, square, in a plaid shirt, walking away purposefully. Getting away—again.

"Scott!" I called. I followed, pushing through the teenagers who had doubled back and stopped to discuss something.

"Bitch," one of them said, and they moved together to block me.

I hurried around them. Where was he? I rushed forward. A plaid shirt, for God's sake! He never used to wear plaid. And he was here at the stupid megamall? He'd wanted freedom to come here?

The plaid shirt and balding head bobbed in the crowd a few yards ahead of me. "Scott!" I called again.

The crush of people lightened outside Legoland as families peeled off to take a break and play with the block displays. Plaid Shirt knelt down to tie his shoe. He stood, checked his watch, turned, and faced me.

Not Scott.

The stranger noticed me looking at him, took in my expression, and spoke. "You okay?"

I breathed again. "I'm fine." Someone passed behind me, knocking my shoulder. "I was looking for someone."

"Mommy!" a child whined.

Oh, cripes. I wheeled around. Where was Hannah?

At least a thousand people were jammed together between this spot and where I'd last seen her.

I hurried back, calling her name, stopping and rising on my toes, trying to see, cursing my height.

"Hannah!"

People stared at me. "Can I help?" I heard as I pushed my way back toward the mine ride. Some people looked disdainful: A lost child? How careless.

I found her exactly where I'd left her outside the mine-ride exit. She'd dropped her bags at her feet and was hugging herself. She looked fierce.

"Arden," she bellowed when she saw me. I went down on my knees and hugged her. It was a one-way hug; she was mad. "Where did you go?" she said. Her fragile, smooth-skinned six-year-old jaw was clenched. "You got away. I stayed here. I wouldn't move. People pushed, but I stayed here."

"That was just right, Hannah. You did just right. I'm sorry."

"You lost me."

"I found you."

"Where did you go? What were you doing? I was scared. People pushed."

"I got swept away."

"You lost me."

"I didn't lose you, Hannah, I didn't lose you."

She collapsed into my arms then. "Where did you go?" she wailed.

"I was looking at someone. Just looking. I wouldn't lose you." Not this, I whispered to myself, feeling her arms squeeze hard; I won't lose this.

"Stop it," she said. "You stop looking!"

"I will," I said, smoothing her hair. "I promise. I'll stop looking."

"Rose Vanaci, Investigator."

"This is Arden Munro."

"Sweetheart, how wonderful you called! I was just typing the weekly report. Nothing good, of course; I'd have called you, but I'm sharing some interesting things I've learned about a man in Minneapolis who counterfeits green cards. Not that it involves your brother, of course, but thanks to Phantom Scott I've got some helpful contacts for a few other skips I'm working on."

"I've decided that I want you to stop looking for him."

I could hear the soft *whoosh* of a chair cushion; she'd probably just sat down and leaned back.

"Are you sure?"

"I am."

"You're the boss. I was just about to begin follow-up

calls to the faxes I sent to all the area motels and rent-a-mailbox stores. Memories are cold by now, but with patience we—"

"Don't bother. I feel like I don't care anymore. He's gone. I know he's out there somewhere, but he's gone. I want to stop looking."

"I'll type this up as a final report, then. I'm sorry. I hate to be unsuccessful. I'm good at what I do, Arden, maybe the best. But I can't perform miracles."

"Now I want something else, and it shouldn't take a miracle."

"Yes?"

"The rest of the fee I was allotted . . . I want to pay you for a different search. I want you to find my parents. I've given you their birth dates and some other background information. I've given you what I know."

She inhaled, taking a low, slow breath. "But they *are* dead."

"Of course they are. I meant that I want you to track down their lives. Everything you can find out about them. That's what I want."

"Wonderful idea," she said. "This will be fun."

I heard tapping on a keyboard. She was probably already starting a new file: Elizabeth Cahill and Conner Munro, dead and missing.

Dead to the world. Missed by me.

PART 3

I can't deny I'm a small-town girl. After just a few hours spent observing the slow flow of gawkers and shoppers at the Farmer's Market around the capitol square, I'd seen plenty I'd never seen in Penokee.

For example? Well, weird body piercing. Even in the backwoods of northern Wisconsin, pierced nipples, eyebrows, lips, and tongues are not unusual. But until visiting Madison, I'd never seen a pierced hand. More accurately, what I saw were several hoops the size of quarters pierced through the flange between the thumb and forefinger on a man's right hand.

I ask you, does this hamper typing speed?

Then there were the two women who were trading off nursing babies, the brigade of acrobatic cheeseheads performing on the capitol steps, a balloon artist who specialized in constructing hot-pink endangered animals, and a woodcarver who fashioned lovely whistles and gave them away with safe-sex brochures.

Madison, Wisconsin: sixty-four square miles surrounded by reality.

My reality was a fresh sunburn. That and the fact that I had now apparently concluded my career as chauffeur and straight guy for the world's best fraternal-twin juggling duo. Kady and Jean had followed the cheesehead brigade as the hired entertainment and were doing their usual postshow autographing in the middle of a crowd of sticky, hot children. I had just finished my usual postshow equipment inventory and packing. Nice to be of service.

I'd finished summer school in early July, and we'd been off and on the road since then. Madison was our eleventh gig in four weeks and the last ever. I hadn't meant to be doing this. I even recalled telling them "no way." But that was during the winter, and when I found out in May that Kady had gone ahead and sent their applications in and they'd been accepted for several jobs, I couldn't refuse the request to drive. I owed them at least that as I'd sure done my best at rearranging their lives over the winter; worse, I'd forgotten to give either of them a graduation present.

"All done?" I asked hopefully when they dragged themselves over to where I was guarding the red cases of paraphernalia.

"One of the little wretches ripped my sleeve," snapped Jean.

"It can be fixed, it's on the seam," consoled her sister.

"Why bother? I won't need it again."

"Best show ever!" I said, sprinkling cheer wherever I went.

"You say that every time," Jean said. "I wish you'd stop."

A pigeon swooped down, landed, and waddled determinedly toward my feet. I curled my toes into the leather of my sandal. "No snack for you, mister," I shouted, and swatted the air. He cocked his head, eyed me, and pooped.

"That's a sign," said Kady. "I'll find the Chamber guy, get the money, and then let's get out of here." She handed me her autograph pad and pen and walked toward an office building across Pinckney Street.

Jean and I hauled the three cases to the car. The 'Cuda had attracted the usual admiring Neanderthals, and two of them were actually stroking the gleaming hood. When they saw a female unlock the trunk they stood erect, hitched their jeans, and grinned.

"Nice car," said the redhead.

"My grandmother's," I answered. "So long, now."

"Maybe we could all go for a drive," said the blond.

"Grandma wouldn't be happy; she needs it back for a nursing-home outing. Good-bye, boys."

They took the hint and left, though they might have turned on a dime if they'd seen what happened next. "Wretched audience, wretched day," Jean said. She dumped the case she was carrying into the trunk, then peeled off her billowy red blouse and bloomers.

"What are you doing stripping in public?" I screeched. "I just got rid of those guys."

"It's hot, I'm sweaty, I've got shorts on, and this is a sports bra; plenty of women are wearing less."

I tried to hustle her into the car, but she resisted. Sensibly, I had to admit, as the interior was dangerously hot after three hours in the sun. I'd wanted to leave the top down, but had learned my lesson during the gig in Spooner, when every bird in the area had left a flyover message on the seats.

Kady sprinted toward us, smiling and waving an envelope. She pulled up when she saw us leaning against the car and not speaking to each other. "What's wrong?" she said.

I tipped my head toward her sister. "We have an attitude."

"Attitude I can handle, but not nudity. C'mon, Jean, I can just see the headline: 'Children's Act Arrested for Indecent Exposure.' "

Jean flipped off her sister and swore under her breath.

"That's pleasant," said Kady. "What do you say we find an ATM so I can deposit this, then get an early supper before we leave?"

I nodded, but before I could speak, Jean pounded on the car's hood. "It's just that it's over," she said. "The thing I most love to do is finished. We'll never do this again, Kady."

"Sure we will. I'll be home at Christmas. You can book something."

"We wouldn't be any good. How can we practice when you're in California and I'm down here at school? Admit it now: It's over."

For once, Kady had no answer. It was over.

Jean pulled on a T-shirt and we started down to the State Street mall, disagreeing on every restaurant we saw. Fifteen minutes later we'd passed up Himalayan, Vietnamese, French, and Italian food and were buying hot dogs for me and salads for them from a vendor on the student union terrace at the university. We sat at a table overlooking a lake.

Kady lifted a limp piece of lettuce, then dropped it to slap at a mosquito. "I sure am glad we did this instead of sitting in a cool restaurant."

I didn't mind; the view was great and my hot dogs were delicious. Jean, her head buried in a day-old newspaper she'd found on the table, seemed not to hear; then she snapped the paper closed. "I don't believe this."

"What?" I asked.

She slumped in her seat and closed her eyes. "I've got to go."

"Go where?" Kady asked.

Jean opened the paper and handed it to her sister. "Look at that: Michael Moschen, two shows tomorrow in Chicago."

"No lie?" Kady pushed her salad aside and reached for the newspaper. "Where does it say? Oh, I see it." She scanned the article, then set the paper down. "That would be some show. Too bad we can't go."

I took it and tried to spot the item that had excited them.

"Who says we can't?" Jean said. "Chicago isn't far."

"No way, Jean."

"Why not? Kady, it's *Michael Moschen*."

"I'd love to see him as much as you would, but we're supposed to go home. They expect us."

"I'm clueless," I chirped. "I can't find it here. Who's Michael Mo-shun?"

Jean glared at her sister but spoke to me. "Just the world's best juggler. A solo act. He's perfect, he's beyond human."

"We saw a documentary on him a couple of years ago," Kady explained. "It was almost depressing, he was so good."

"I need to get you two home," I said. "I promised. It may not be far to Chicago, but it eats up two more days. Besides, I've never driven in that big a city, *and* I have to pick up Hannah at the airport when she flies in from Phoenix."

"That's not until Tuesday," said Jean. "Plenty of time. I want to do this, you guys."

"We can't," said Kady.

I sat back and started on my second hot dog. Let them fight it out.

"I want to do this," Jean repeated. "For once in my life, I really want something. Usually it's laid-back Jean who always gives in and lets you two have your way. Kady the boss and Arden the spoiled orphan; you guys always get what you want. Now it's my turn. And I want this."

"It means at least one extra night in a hotel and gas and food," said Kady. "That'll blow what we earned today."

"I don't care."

Kady looked at me. I shrugged. Jean had a point about who usually won. So, let her have one.

"Then you have to call Mom and Dad," Kady said to her sister. "We're expected home tonight."

"You," said Jean. "You're so much better at that sort of thing."

"No way. This is your scheme, so you do the dirty work."

The same thought hit them both at the same instant

and their faces, one round and sunburned, one long and tan, turned to me.

"Why not?" I said, already digging out my long-distance calling card. "After all, they always liked me best."

If you do it just right you can cruise through a toll without stopping. The trick is in how and when you toss the change into the machine. If you do it too soon, you miss and have to try again. Throw too hard and the coins bounce around too long on their way down. A soft toss means they slide down the chute in slo-mo. But with the right toss out the window, the coins are gulped and the booth arm lifts before the speedometer hits zero.

I had perfected this skill by the third tollbooth on the Illinois toll road. Of course it helped to be driving a convertible with the top down; my wide overhand lob was the key.

After about three hours of sixty-five miles per hour, however, my coin-tossing was the only thing served by having the top down. I was burned to a crisp, Kady had gotten something in her eye, Jean had let the map blow away, and we all had highway hair.

The road we were on got busier, wider, more complicated. Traffic sped by and around us. We were three girls in a convertible and obviously people felt free to establish contact. They waved, we were mooned, and one carload of clowns pulled alongside and tossed trash into our backseat, splattering Jean with warm soda. "I don't like this," I shouted to the twins. "It will be dark soon, we'll be hitting the city, I can't handle it if things get any friendlier. To top it off, we don't know where we're going."

Kady cupped her ear and shook her head. Odd that she couldn't hear me because we could both hear Jean, in the back, swearing as she wiped off the soda.

I peeled off onto the exit ramp for an oasis and pulled in next to a van filling up with children. "Cool car," one of them said between licks of an ice-cream cone.

"Hands off," I answered as I put the top up.

As we walked toward the oasis restaurant I looked back and saw the little wretch leave a creamy handprint on the car.

"We need a plan," I said as we slid into a booth with our suppers. "I'm all for spontaneity, but what we're doing suddenly seems stupid. I especially do not want to hit a huge, strange downtown on a Saturday night and cruise up and down looking for a hotel."

"Then we get one along the way and go downtown tomorrow," said Kady.

"Where along the way?"

Kady thought. "Let's look for an airport."

A plane was taking off overhead as we exited the oasis complex. No motel walls could block out that noise, but I suspected I'd sleep through anything; we'd left Penokee at six A.M. and I was dead.

The vanload of children was gone, but my car had

attracted another audience—at least a dozen adults were crowded around the 'Cuda.

"Is this yours?" a tall middle-aged woman with Dutch-girl braids said as I approached, keys dangling from my fist. "It's just gorgeous. Love the power-bulge hood. Is it original?"

"I'm not sure," I said as I unlocked the car. People stepped back. "It's really my brother's."

"You going to 'Cuda Con?" said Dutch Girl.

The twins and I exchanged glances. " 'Cuda Con?" I asked.

"The international car show is going on in Chicago this weekend. 'Cuda Con is sort of a subgroup. Barracuda convention, get it? That's where we're going. It's an annual caravan. Three of us left Dallas two days ago, and we've been picking up cars and drivers ever since." She thumbed behind her and the 'Cuda crowd parted, revealing several beautifully restored Barracudas parked on the tarmac outside the oasis.

"Are you headed into the city, possibly somewhere near the lake?" asked Jean.

Dutch Girl nodded. "Hilton."

Jean and Kady eyed each other, then looked at me. I shrugged. "Do you mind," Jean asked, "if we ride along?"

Dutch Girl and the others in the caravan made their pit stop; then we all rolled out together, a long line of muscle cars headed toward the giant city on the inland sea.

"What a view!" Kady pulled back the curtains and let in the sun. I rolled over. Jean threw a pillow at her sister.

"Hundred and thirty a night, there better be a view," I grumbled. "One of you snored. Who was it?"

"Must have been your dream," Jean said. "What time is it?"

"Nearly noon," said Kady. "You two deadheads slept through three phone calls. I told you not to watch that late movie."

"Who called?"

"The concierge called about the show tickets; they're holding matinee seats at the box office window. Mom called and said she got the message and she's happy we're staying someplace nice."

I opened the minibar, grabbed a muffin, and checked the price list as I unwrapped it and took a bite. Five bucks. "She has no idea how nice," I said.

"And Beverly called," Kady continued. Beverly was Dutch Girl, our protector. "She twisted arms at the front desk and they're letting us have a late checkout. Arden, she also said that you should call her by noon if you want to go to the car show with her." She eyed me suspiciously. "What did you tell her?"

"Nothing."

"Are you going to 'Cuda Con, maybe just to look around?"

I opened a container of orange juice. Four bucks. "Why would I want to do that?"

Jean slid out of bed and stretched. "Underwear dry?" she asked her sister.

"Thanks to me, yes. Lucky there was a blow-dryer."

"Oh, listen to the martyr: She had to dry the underwear."

They wrestled verbally some more, but I tuned it out, a polished skill. Besides, I was ready for another five-dollar muffin.

Back home in Penokee, Wisconsin, I could pull off cool, no problem. But in Chicago I was obviously small-town stupid on the loose. Leaving the hotel with my neck ratcheted back several degrees so I could gawk at the skyline, I walked off the curb and nearly got slapped onto the hood of a speeding taxi. Then, always the eager beaver, I stood first in the pack waiting to board a bus headed uptown. Its door swung open abruptly, nearly knocking me over, and I got pushed back by a horde of exiting riders. I tripped going up the steps and dropped my fare. The bus lurched forward and I toppled into a seat, nearly landing in a woman's lap.

She tipped her head toward me and looked at Kady. "Where she from?" she asked, a honeyed accent to her English.

My friend sighed wearily. "Wisconsin."

The woman nodded. Uh-huh.

"I don't feel good about this," said Kady. "Please come to the show with us. I guarantee you'll enjoy it."

"I don't care how good this guy is, I've seen enough juggling for a lifetime."

"You can't wander the streets of Chicago by yourself."

"I certainly can, but I don't plan to." I pointed toward the massive building looming behind the theater. "I'll go in the Art Institute; that's safe enough and I should be able to find plenty to hold my interest for a few hours."

Kady appeared ready to debate more, but Jean intervened with a firm tug on her sister's sleeve. "Let her loose," she said. "It's almost showtime."

Kady nodded and pointed to the theater's doors. "We meet right here in two hours."

Two hours—ha! The minute I walked into the museum I knew I'd need two lifetimes to see everything. The place was huge.

Way too huge for the sulky little guy I encountered by the rack of guide brochures. He swatted the bootee-bound feet of an infant sibling dozing in a stroller while his parents studied gallery maps.

"Cool place, huh?" I said to him. "Did you see the lions outside?" He tossed a sullen glance my way and then swatted the baby harder. I leaned down. "I'm guessing that the best thing to do in a place like this," I whispered, "is count all the pictures with naked bodies."

His hand froze midswat as he stared at me. I could see a giggle rising and I turned and fled.

I'd been to plenty of museums in my life. There was the fishing museum in Hayward, the hat museum in Ripon, the farm implement museum in Trempealeau, the shoe museum in Des Moines, the underwear museum in Worthington. All respectable landmarks of Midwestern culture, but I don't recall that any of those places rendered me awestruck and woozy. And after only an hour of picture gazing, I was clearly woozy.

"Those Impressionists sure could paint," I murmured to a mink-wrapped woman planted in front of a Monet.

She nodded. "To say the least." She eyed my earrings (modified fishing bobbers), my newest bowling shirt ("Hubie"), my too-many-days-on-the-road personal grooming. "First impressions are dangerous, dear, but I might have taken you for more of an Abstract Expressionist fan."

"Headed that way now," I replied cheerfully, and turned, as if I knew where I was going, to walk through the labyrinth of hallways and galleries. I edged around a tour group as a family hurried out of a gallery. Mom pushed the stroller fiercely, while Dad walked with a boy slung over his shoulder. The boy was laughing hysterically.

My sullen little friend, only something had cheered him immeasurably.

"Stop it," growled his father. "Stop laughing."

The boy spotted me. "I got up to thirty-three," he gasped as his family resumed their hurried exit. He pointed. "The one in there's the best!"

It was the best. Matisse, *Bathers by a River*. A huge thing with four naked forms, black strokes on green, gray, and blue. It had driven the little guy to hysteria, but it muted me. I sat down to stare.

I snapped out of it when the mink glided into my view. "Nice, yes?" the woman said. "But I hate the frame; it's the only one I notice in the entire museum; absolutely wrong." Mink glided away.

Once again, illumination. The frames. Evidently the good ones shouldn't be noticed, and I hadn't. I'd spent over an hour gawking at great pictures and hadn't noticed a single frame.

So long, ArdenArt. Why burn the creative juices to prop up someone else's work? No way I wanted to keep on making frames for other people's pictures, drawings, and faces. Surrounded by some of the world's best art, I knew what I wanted to do: make the stuff that goes on the inside.

A bit shaken by this personal revelation and upheaval, I did what anyone would do: hit the gift shop. When Hannah had last called home she'd warned me she was bringing presents from Arizona, so maybe it wouldn't hurt to do the same from my impromptu trip to Chicago.

A mobile for the nursery, a Cassatt print of a mother and child for Claire, a necklace for Hannah. I debated buying some onyx-and-silver earrings for Jace. He'd need just one, of course, but spares are always nice. They were gorgeous, but I worried that they might be too personal and expensive a gift for a recently revived long-distance thing.

"Handsome studs," a clerk said, appearing out of nowhere to monitor my browsing.

"Wrong word choice," I replied, and decided to get Jace a T-shirt.

"How was the show?"

Jean leaned against the theater wall. "Wonderful," she whispered. "Stupendous, sexy, out of this world, beautiful."

I set my shopping bag down and turned to Kady. "Did she say sexy?"

Kady nodded. "She did. My sister has this thing about guys wearing bodysuits. We bought you a souvenir." She pulled three large cube-shaped beanbags out of her backpack. "The yellow one's autographed."

"For me?" I said skeptically.

"Fine, then; I'll keep them. If you change your mind, you can have Jean's."

"It was truly humbling," said Jean. "I may never juggle again. Why should I? I've now seen the best and why should I bother? Never again."

"Fat chance," I said to Kady.

She nodded. "I bet she doesn't last half an hour before she's tossing something."

It took twenty minutes. We walked into the lakeside park, where we joined the slow-moving promenade. A few blocks away, near a huge pink fountain guarded by garish gold statues, we bought some food from a vendor and found places to sit and eat. The skyline loomed, gray and dark, shadowed by a few low clouds.

A little boy trying to keep up with his parents stumbled on the concrete and scraped his knee. He sat, held it, and bawled. His mother coaxed him to rise. No luck. He just screamed louder, and his baby sibling joined in. The sunburned parents exchanged exhausted looks. The dad shifted a diaper bag to a different shoulder and rocked the stroller. Jean reached into her sister's purse, pulled out her souvenir beanbags, and began tossing the colorful cubes up and down. Kady nudged me and we both smiled. That's when I checked my watch. Twenty minutes.

The boy stopped crying and stared at Jean. She puffed her cheeks and made a face. He smiled. Without taking her eyes off him she tossed a bag to her sister, who automatically caught the cube and fed it back. Within a moment Kady had her own cubes flying, and the show began.

"Don't you dare put out a hat for money," I warned as I rose with our garbage. "It's probably illegal here and I sure don't have the cash to bail you out of a Chicago jail."

The nearest trash bin was overflowing. Gulls pecked at the spillage. Good citizen from a small town, I started picking up the mess and smashing it into the bin. A blader whizzed by, tossed a drink cup stuffed with wrappers. He rolled on out of sight as his trash hit the ground. "Slob!" I shouted, and at least fifty people turned and looked at me.

A crowd of children and weary parents had gathered around Kady and Jean. It was hard to tell who was happier—the kids or their parents, who were obviously thrilled to have someone else entertain the children. I couldn't see the show but I heard the silly noises:

Kady's "ugh, ugh" and Jean's "gotcha, baby," followed by plenty of cheers from the audience.

Behind them, Lake Michigan was a placid gray sheet. I stared at the water until my eyes blinked and teared, then looked back at the people surrounding my friends. There were even more now—children galore, mothers and fathers, a few scoffing kids my own age, one policeman, and a few yards back, alone, a man in a blue dress shirt and jeans. Short guy, kind of bald, tan, no beard.

There he was.

Scott leaned forward, peering in disbelief at the crowd, stunned to recognize the performers, his carefree day in Chicago now ruined. Then he looked around, a startled deer. Could he still get away, had he been seen?

I pounced on him before he took a step. Sprang from behind and pounded him on the back.

"You bastard! I should kill you! I knew it, I knew it, I knew it."

He sank under my punches. "Oh, God," he said. "Oh, God," he murmured again and again, maybe ten times more. I didn't quit hitting.

"Stop it," he said finally, wearily.

"Like hell I will. I hate you, I hate you. How stupid did you think I was?"

I felt someone tugging on my arm. Jean pulled me away just as the policeman put a hand on Scott. The juggling was over and the crowd had turned, all eyes on me and my brother. Parents began to hurry away with their young, while the kids my age stayed and watched. *This is better!* their faces said.

"None of this," the policeman said.

"You heard him, Arden," Scott said. "Cool off, now."

"Just a brother-sister thing, Officer," Kady explained. "She's very mad at him. She hasn't seen him for a long time. He forgot to write. That's all."

The policeman wasn't so sure. "That right, miss?"

I nodded, but kept my eyes on my brother.

The cop patted the air with his hand. "Everything okay now?"

"Just fine," I snapped, eyes still on my brother. The cop left.

"What are you doing here?" Scott said.

"What am *I* doing here? You're the one who's supposed to be dead."

"Shhh," Jean cautioned. "You're getting loud again."

"Arden," said Kady, "I am very, very sorry. Huge apology, okay? None of us should ever have doubted you."

"So I fooled someone?" Scott said.

"We all thought you were dead," Kady said. "Thought you were frozen solid under the ice. Not Arden, though. She insisted it was all a stinky stunt."

Scott lifted a hand and reached for me. "I knew it would work if I could just fool Arden. I knew that would be the tough part."

I backed away from him. "Stop it, dead man; I don't want to listen to you." I walked to the nearest empty bench, sat down, pulled my knees into my arms and glared at him. Kady followed, ready to nurse if I collapsed. Jean stayed with Scott, ready to chase if he bolted.

"Should I call someone?" Kady asked me.

"No."

"Al or John, maybe. Or Claire. They've got to know."

"They will, but I get to tell them."

Scott stuffed his hands into his pockets, looked around, shuffled nervously, watched me. He picked up some litter, walked it to a trash barrel, then came over to me. Jean followed him closely.

"What are you doing?" he said to her.

"Making sure you don't get away."

He motioned toward the bench. "May I?" he asked Kady. She nodded and gave him her spot. He sat, placed a hand on my knee, and said, "So, Arden, how were your grades?"

I couldn't help it, I collapsed and cried. Fell against his shoulder and emptied months of pent-up tears and snot on his shirt.

"Give us some time?" he asked the twins.

"Arden?" Jean said.

"It's okay," I said. "He's not going anywhere."

Kady nodded. "We'll go hunt down some ice cream."

"We'll be right here," I said as I wiped my face on his shirtsleeve.

Scott leaned back. "Yuck."

"Oh, I am so sorry, I am sooo sorry: I messed up your shirt, what an awful thing to do to someone. Can you ever forgive me?" I turned away from him and looked at the thousands of joyful summer-happy faces. My brother was back from the dead; wasn't that how I was supposed to feel?

"How's Claire?"

I snorted. "You care?"

"I do."

"She's fine. About to be a mother again, but you know that. She's getting so big it looks like she could pop any day. By the way, they've moved into the house."

"What?"

"Last month. I had all that room, they were cramped out at the park, she'll need help with the two kids, and who better than the baby's aunt. *Especially* since the father isn't around." A smile spread across his face, and he turned away to hide it. "What's the joke, Scott?" I snapped. "I don't see anything funny about any of this."

"I'm just enjoying the predictability of things, I guess."

"What do you mean?"

"Arden, without you I couldn't have done it. The conscience would have pricked too hard. But I knew you'd come through, knew you'd do the right thing for Claire. Be responsible, step in, take care of things." He shifted and stretched his legs. "Like I did for you."

The jazzy sound of a clarinet floated across the air. Five minutes passed without either of us speaking, then:

"Are you okay, Arden?"

"I had an awful winter, Scott."

"I'm sorry."

"I looked so hard for you. They all thought I was having some sort of a breakdown, but I wasn't. I knew what you had done." I punched his shoulder again, harder than ever.

"Careful," he said. "Cop might be hovering."

"It was too perfect. You did it too perfectly. Did you have fun planning it?"

"I did, I must admit. But it was scary, in a way. Almost changed my mind every day."

"I didn't know right away. For weeks I was pretty shocked about you dying. Then I woke up and I could practically smell it. From almost the moment Claire told me she was pregnant it felt like I'd been shaken out of a bad dream. But no one would take me seriously. It will feel so good to tell them. How did you do it, exactly? I figured you dumped the sled and walked through the woods, but how did you plan it, how did you get away, how did you live?"

He took a breath, stroked the phantom beard and then let go of his secret in a long jumbled rush, as if he was happy to be sharing it with someone at last. He told me about his trips to Minneapolis, supposedly to buy a new machine, and he'd done that, yes, but he'd also set up a mailbox at a packaging store, then bought an ID, car, and trailer from a guy he knew who specialized in what he called difficult transactions. "The guy can get anything," Scott said, still amazed.

"Is your car stolen?"

"Don't think so. The papers look good, they're all in the right name."

"You could be in serious legal trouble, Scott. The county won't be happy that they staged a dangerous and unnecessary search."

"It won't be anything I can't face. I prepared for that too, Arden, for getting caught. I checked into the legal crap; there's nothing too serious they can slap on me. If I get hauled back to Wisconsin and put in front of a judge, I suppose I could claim emotional duress and insanity. Take my chances."

"You don't look very duressed. Nice tan. Where have you been for six months?"

"Around. Warm places. I drove to the Grand Canyon, Las Vegas, Florida. Take a look at this." He showed me a Minnesota license for Phil Owen. The picture was Scott.

"You can quit pretending to be him."

"I suppose. That will be nice, in a way. I was never quite sure how good the bogus identity was. Always worried I'd get stopped by a cop for something and he'd run the name through a computer and Bang! I'd find out Phil Owen was some dead mugging victim, or maybe a wanted career criminal. America's Most Wanted. Well, I knew he wasn't that. I actually went to a post office in Nevada once and checked the posters. Did they ever find my wallet in the river?"

"They found everything but you."

"I've been carrying an old license with me. In case I had an accident somewhere, I wanted you to be notified."

"How thoughtful, considering I was supposed to think you were already dead."

He shrugged, then continued his story. "The same

guy delivered the car to Penokee and left it at the motel. There was a rally that weekend, and the motel lot was filled with cars and trailers. That's why I picked that date—if anyone had seen me, I would have been forgettable, just another sledder. Besides, the rally diverted most of the sledders to the track at Brimhall, so I didn't think I'd see anyone on the state trail. I rode to the motel early that last morning, put the sled on the trailer, and drove out to the river. I parked the car, got back on the sled, and was back home before you were out of bed. Later that day I rode to Winker's, had some beers, and then off I went in the storm. I dumped the trailer in a lot in Rice Lake."

"Your car's a big old beater, right? People saw you, Scott, they saw it parked on JG."

"It's a new Camry, and I parked it on TT. It's a longer distance from the river to that road, but there's not as much traffic on TT. It was snowing hard and I was on snowshoes. Not getting me on those ever again." He shook his head. "Arden, people may have seen someone, but it wasn't me. I was careful and I was ready to give it up at any time if *anything* went wrong."

I stretched my legs. "I had it," I muttered. "I had the big picture figured right, I just didn't get the details. I'll have to tell Rose."

"Who's Rose?"

"An investigator I hired."

"A detective? How much money did you spend?"

"No more than you were worth, okay? And speaking of money, where did you get it? That's the one thing I couldn't figure out. How could you afford to buy this new life?"

He sighed. "I need a Sno-Kone. Want one?"

"Blue, please."

I watched him take his turn at the vendor's cart. Cone by cone, he moved up in line. An older couple right in front of him took a very long time deciding on flavors, and he turned and smiled at me, his eyebrows hopping on his broad forehead as he tipped his head toward the old people. At that moment my rage subsided, cooled by the gust of lake air that washed over me.

"I don't know how long it will last," I said when he handed me my Sno-Kone, "but at this moment I'm glad to see you."

"You were always happiest when I brought home the groceries. By the way, have you been eating okay? You're very thin."

Not thin, not by a stretch. I had lost a few pounds, maybe ten. I filled my mouth with slush. "I've been on the Anxiety Diet. Now tell me about the money."

"You're so smart, you can figure it out."

"No one could."

"You will."

My bad mood returned and I swore sharply. "I am tired of your game, Scott. Where did you get the money? Did you steal it?"

"Not really. Maybe from you, I guess. But you and the future baby got everything else, so I figured I was entitled to what I took."

"What did you take? I checked your baseball cards. They weren't worth much."

"No," he said thoughtfully, "I mostly collected no-names. Utility guys, not the stars."

"The money?"

"Mom and Dad left a very nice photography collection. She'd started collecting when she was in college, building on a few pieces that belonged to her parents. I'd almost forgotten about it, because we stashed all that stuff in the basement years ago. There were some pretty valuable things. Stieglitz, Steichen, Man Ray, Arbus. I sold the collection in Minneapolis when I was buying the sled. Figured no one would know the difference because Mom and Dad's estate was handled by some senile guy down in Rice Lake, things weren't inventoried very carefully, and I didn't think you'd remember we had them."

"I didn't."

"I didn't sell all the pictures. I left you two. They're packed in a box tucked under the steps, behind the trunks."

"How thoughtful. Did it ever occur to you how awful it would be for the rest of us to lose you?"

"Of course it did. I guess I decided not to think about that, not to let it be a factor. Arden, for ten years I was the good guy. Reliable, steady Scott. Day after day, year after year, it was all I heard. 'Take a look at my engine, Scott.' 'I'm having trouble with my brakes, Scott.' 'Aren't you sweet with your sister, Scott.' 'Isn't Arden clever, Scott?' Shit. Did people ever wonder what I was feeling? Nope, I was just the perfect mechanic, the dutiful brother, and God knows I was the obedient son. Hell, it went back longer than ten years. Our parents were great people, Arden, and sure, I loved them, but, man, how they pushed! They pushed me through school, wanting perfect grades. Pushed me to

Yale. Pushed and pushed while we moved to new places so they could play out dreams of being saintly doctors. Just when I got old enough to think about pushing back, they died and I had to take care of you. Then, just when I was beginning to think I was done playing Daddy, Claire laid her news on me. I couldn't do it, Arden. I didn't have it in me. I had to get out, had to go after what I wanted." A frail-looking green bug landed on his knee and he flicked it away. "I know there's no way you could understand."

"Maybe I do. You were . . . tired of being the frame for my art."

He laughed, a familiar little nasal rush of air. "Curious analogy, but close enough. Thanks for trying."

"No . . ." Yeeps, why was this so hard? "Thank you."

"For what?"

"For earlier. For taking care of me all that time. I do know it was hard. Thank you."

I thought then of him sitting on my bed so long ago, holding me after one of my nightmares. Whispering, "I have dreams too, I have them too."

I'd always thought he meant that he'd shared the nightmares, but maybe he didn't. Maybe he'd meant just what he said—I have dreams too.

"Might as well tell me, brother—what were these great unfulfilled dreams that inspired you to leave everything?"

"That's the thing, Arden; I didn't have a clue."

The paper cup dripped syrup on my hand. I licked it clean and crumpled the cone, rose, and tossed it into a nearby trash can. He smiled when I sat back down, lifted my hand and kissed it, the only time I could remember he'd ever done something like that.

"So I fooled everyone but you."

"Don't be proud, okay? A lot of people cared about you, so when they thought you'd gone for a last swim in the icy river, they were shocked silly and couldn't think beyond that. You owe everyone a huge apology."

"Tell them I'm sorry."

"You can do it when you come back."

He cocked his head and shrugged his shoulders. Swatted at something.

"You are coming back, aren't you? Scott? Are you going to make me call the police and have them deal with you?"

"Not sure they'd find reason to. Besides, you wouldn't do that."

"I would. Your baby's about to be born. You've got to."

"I don't 'got to' do anything. I am done with the 'got to.' " He roughed up his hair with his hands, then clasped them behind his head. "What I did was not entirely selfish, Arden."

"Spare me."

"The way I was feeling . . . it made sense to me that it was better for the baby to have a dead father than a deranged one."

"Why didn't you just tell someone you were going nuts? It's not that hard to ask for help."

"Habit, I guess; just never dared."

"That's silly."

"You think so? Arden, all those early years I was in charge—a single guy, right?—if I had shown a moment's weakness or confusion, they would have packed you up and sent you off in a flash."

"Maybe they should have."

He gripped my shoulder and turned me toward him. "Do you really think so?"

I picked off his hand and sagged. "No."

"Okay then, I'll ask: Will you help me with this? People will take their cue from you."

"You come home with me, Scott, and we'll see what happens. I suppose I might help you whine to a judge, if you have to. But I'd be doing it for Claire and Hannah and the baby. And any money they want you to pay for the bogus search comes out of your stash. Where is it, anyway? You don't carry all that cash, do you?"

"It's in a safe-deposit box in Minneapolis. I go back now and then."

"Wasn't that risky?"

"Maybe I wanted to be found. You think?"

"I don't know what to think."

Kady and Jean reappeared, sensed we weren't ready for company, then disappeared behind the fountain with their sundaes.

"You really hired a detective?"

"I did, but then I quit caring and took her off your case and had her look for Mom and Dad."

"In Honduras? Arden, that's weird; they're long past finding."

"I hired her to look for their lives. You were gone, so how else was I supposed to know about them?"

"I did feel bad about that. I may have had my arguments with them, but I realized you deserved to know more about our parents and I hadn't told you very much."

"No fooling. I couldn't believe some of the stuff she found out: miscarriages, Dad was married before, filthy rich grandparents, a crazy aunt who died in a mental hospital. God, Scott, didn't we *ever* talk? How could you not tell me these things? You should have told me everything about them the moment we knew they were dead. Bad enough to be an orphan, brother, but I lost a lot more because you didn't talk to me."

"You were six, Arden, and I was nineteen. Bedtime stories about suicide and miscarriages might not have been a good idea, okay? Besides, it took everything I had in me just to get you up and dressed and off to school, day after day after day. So, no, we didn't talk. But you know it all now."

"I don't know it all. There are some gaps, like around the time when I was born. Rose couldn't find any friends who knew anything about them."

"Not surprised, really. We'd just moved to Milwaukee. They'd practiced for a few years in a free clinic in St. Louis, then decided to do surgical residencies. We lived in married-student housing and most of the neighbors were foreign students. They've probably all gone back to their home countries now." He shifted onto his left hip and faced me. "I guess that makes me the only person in the whole wide world who remembers the day you were born."

"And that's the only reason in the whole wide world I might ever forgive you for disappearing."

A couple stopped and embraced a few feet in front of us, then swayed to some internal music.

"Do you suppose Claire will ever forgive me?" he asked.

"I have no idea."

A sax player had put out a hat a few yards away. He closed his eyes and played a sad, winding melody, then paused while a woman companion postured and shouted a few lines of poetry. A small crowd gathered around them. The sax played again, then more poetry.

My brother looked tired. Maybe life on the loose wasn't as fun as he'd convinced himself it would be. He looked older and heavier, probably the result of six months of sitting in a car and eating drive-through meals.

"Why are you in Chicago?" he asked as the sax played.

"We were in Madison. Jean and Kady were doing a show and they found out that the world's best juggler was giving a performance here. We drove on down. I bet I know why you're here."

"Tell me."

"The car show. Were you there?"

"Haven't been near the place. Didn't know about it, and I doubt I'd have gone. Too big a chance I'd see someone I know."

"Then why Chicago?"

He smiled. "I guess you could say I came to see our parents."

"What do you mean?"

"Years ago they had this artist friend, Harry. Did your detective find out about him?"

I tipped my head back and sighed loudly. "No. I thought I'd never know. Harry. Who was he?"

"A college friend of Mom's. A sculptor. Nice guy, he used to show up at the oddest times, always flying in from some strange place."

"Where does he live? Would he talk to me about them?"

"He's dead. AIDS, back in the eighties. They took it real hard. He was mildly famous—in art circles, anyway. He did a piece with their hands cast in bronze. I'd always heard how it was kind of weird. But I guess it was of interest or value to someone because it's part of the collection here at a museum."

"The Art Institute?" I tipped my head in the direction of the giant museum.

"No, a smaller place, just for contemporary art."

Once again I socked him, but I was losing vigor; he barely moved. "Why didn't you tell me I could go to a museum and see their hands? Why didn't we ever go there together?"

"Because, Miss Hothead, the museum was in name only and didn't have a permanent building. Everything it owned was either loaned out or in storage. Our parents' hands have been in a warehouse for twenty years. But the museum opened a building recently and the permanent collection finally went on display. I read about it in an art magazine when I was in Florida—tanning on the beach, if you must know."

"Did you see it?"

"Yeah. I'd say it's pretty incoherent. The four hands are suspended on wires and they sort of swing around over a muddle of stuff."

"Did you touch it?"

He lifted an eyebrow. "And set off alarms and get hauled away by some guard? No, I didn't touch it."

The performance by the fountain concluded and the poet and saxophonist bowed to the applauding crowd. A few coins and bills were dropped into their hat.

"I like Chicago," Scott said. "It might be nice to stay put and try living in a big city. There's a good art school here, you know. You might want to check that out. I went through its gallery today. Edgy stuff; you'd fit right in." He poked me gently on the shoulder. "Still mad at me?"

"What I feel is so totally new I don't have a word for it. *Pissed* comes the closest. *Disillusioned* works well too."

He sagged a bit and shifted his gaze toward the lake. After a moment he took a deep breath, lifted his arms, and held his wrists together. "I'm your prisoner, sis. Go ahead and cuff me."

We corralled Kady and Jean, returned to the hotel, and booked a second room for the night. "We'll get your stuff from your motel tomorrow," I said to my brother. "I don't trust you out of my sight, so we'll share a room; besides, one of them snores."

We met Beverly in the lobby. She'd just returned from 'Cuda Con and was laden with large plastic bags filled with free automotive samples. I introduced my brother. "He's the one who restored the 'Cuda," I explained.

"Gorgeous car," she replied.

Scott's jaw dropped and he turned to me. "You drove the 'Cuda to Chicago?"

"She's been driving it lots," said Jean. "Never washes it, either."

"Too bad about that big dent on the hood," added Kady.

His pain was palpable. I loved it.

I didn't love making the phone calls, though, which was weird because I had always thought I'd savor the moment I'd be able to say "I told you so." Al and John were pretty cool about it, after the initial honking and sputtering. I couldn't hear, of course, what they said to Scott, but John told me afterward that he'd get right down to the office to start sweeping up the mess. I guess we'd all be doing that in some way or another.

The hardest call was the one to Claire. She wasn't home for hours; then when she finally answered, she sounded beat. "You'd better sit down," I said. "This is going to blow you away."

While they talked, I went to the twins' room and ordered a room-service dinner and a bathrobe to be sent to mine. Then I went back and showered. Scott and Claire were still talking when I finished my steak, so I started on the one I'd ordered for him.

I was halfway through his filet when he handed me the phone. "Your turn."

"You okay?" I asked Claire immediately.

"Oh, sure, just dandy. Arden, I'm sorry I didn't—"

"Forget it. We'll see you tomorrow."

Scott crashed fast and hard. I guess life in a car and cheap motels isn't very restful, especially when you're always looking over your shoulder. I sat in a chair in front of the door and watched him sleep. No way I was going to risk him sneaking out.

At one A.M. I moved to the other bed and crawled under the blankets. Too tired, too full of the day, I could take a chance. Hell—let him run if he wanted. I'd found him, I'd proved my point, I'd gotten what I wanted, I'd said thank you. Case closed, right?

Wrong: my name. I sat up and swung my legs off the bed, then bounced onto his and pounded on his back.

"Wake up. Wake up and tell me," I said as I pummeled him.

He pushed up on his arms and turned a sleep-drugged face toward me. "What?"

"Tell me about my name. You wanted to, that last day, it's how I knew you weren't dead. Tell me."

"Geez, Arden, let me sleep. In the morning."

"Tell me about my name. I came too close to never knowing. I want to hear it now."

He sat up and rubbed his eyes. "It's not much, really. Certainly not worth waking me up for."

"Tell me."

He leaned against the headboard and closed his eyes. "Okay, let's see. I told you we were living in married-student housing back then, right? Mom had taken time off because you were on the way and she wasn't feeling so good. Well, there were all these women living in the complex—it was like a never-ending coffee party that moved from apartment to apartment. One night they were sitting around our kitchen, and Mom was telling everyone about this terrific hand lotion. She had really dry skin from scrubbing up so much, but she'd found this great lotion and to hear her talk you'd think it had saved her life. It was made by Elizabeth Arden. She decided to give you the name because she really loved the stuff. Everyone thought it was so funny and wonderful, they laughed and laughed, a bunch of cackling hens. Her name was Elizabeth, of course, and she wouldn't share that, so you got tagged Arden. And that's the story, little sister. Now may I please go back to sleep? Man, I was having the best dream and now I've lost it. You owe me, sis."

He burrowed into his pillow and crashed again.

I *owed* him?

A shard of moonlight slid through a crack in the drapes and glistened on his pate.

I didn't know what I owed him, but I did know what I'd *give* him: forgiveness; it was cheap enough. And maybe, in the morning, another thank-you. And he could sure have the damn car.

I walked to the window, stood behind the drapes, and looked out. The moon was high and the lake was sheathed in a silver skin.

I'd found my brother and I'd found my name.

Be careful what you wish for.

Arden.

Arden, Arden, Arden. At last I knew the story. Not

exactly the one I'd imagined or hoped for. Okay, so I hadn't been named for someone's favorite fictional character, or a best friend, or a beloved bohemian aunt.

Arden.

I was named for an emollient.

PART 4

"What a beautiful little girl. What's her name?"

"Baby Gap," I answered. Hannah giggled. The gallery guard stiffened, which was a neat trick, considering how stiff they are normally. "It's a nickname, from her initials," I said, flashing an apologetic smile. "Her real name is Gwenyth Arden Poole."

Hannah crossed her arms. "She's named for my mom's mom."

And, of course, *moi*.

I shifted the gorgeous little redhead to my other arm and she immediately started sucking my shoulder. When had she last been fed? Probably just one of those minor details neglected amid the tempest of that day's episode in the continuing saga of her parents' long-distance *thing*. I fished in the diaper bag and felt for a bottle.

"The boss said you came down from Wisconsin," said the guard. "Just for this, or is there a special occasion?" Then her walkie-talkie crackled and she lifted it and listened.

"What shall we tell the lady?" I whispered to Baby Gap as she lunged for the bottle. "That it's the one-month anniversary of Daddy's getting off probation?"

The guard holstered her radio and smiled, still waiting for an answer.

"My brother moved to the city recently," I said politely. "We're visiting."

"And my mom is applying to work in a museum," Hannah said to the guard. "The big one with the dinosaurs. She has an interview today. If she gets the job we might move here and she'd be the" —she took a breath and readied the words—"assistant director of education."

"That's cool, kid." The guard's walkie-talkie commanded her attention again. "Just about set," she said to us. "This is really unprecedented, you know. I've never heard of any museum ever allowing this."

Because they'd never had to deal with me, that's why. I smiled again. "We're very grateful. The curator was so understanding."

Hannah tugged on my arm. "Are you sure I can do it too?"

"Of course, hotshot; you're family."

The guard spoke into the walkie-talkie again, then nodded at me. "Go ahead, but the alarm's off only for a minute. This piece is a crowd favorite and we don't want to attract others."

"No problem."

I lifted my niece's hand and stroked it with my

thumb, then held it out toward the sculpture. A heavy bronze wrist bumped her pink pinkie. "Okay, little one," I whispered into the small ear. "This one is your grandpa, that one is your grandma. Uncurl your fist—good. Here we go. Hold hands."

About the Author

Marsha Qualey has written four previous young adult novels: *Everybody's Daughter*, *Revolutions of the Heart*, *Come In from the Cold*, and *Hometown*. Her books have been included among the ALA's Best Books for Young Adults and Quick Picks, the New York Public Library's Books for the Teen Age, and the *Bulletin*'s and *School Library Journal*'s Best Books of the Year, and she has won two Minnesota Book Awards. The mother of four children, Marsha Qualey lives in Minnesota with her family.